I0752634

THE PATH OF LIFE

STIJN STREUVELS

Translated From The West-Flemish By

ALEXANDER TEIXEIRA DE MATTOS

The Path of Life

Stijn Streuvels

PO Box 2211
Fairfield, IA 52556
www.1stworldlibrary.org
First Edition

LCCN: 2004195680

Softcover ISBN: 1-4218-0493-X
Hardcover ISBN: 1-4218-0393-3
eBook ISBN: 1-4218-0593-6

Purchase *"The Path of Life"*
as a traditional bound book at:
www.1stWorldLibrary.org/purchase.asp?ISBN=1-4218-0493-X

1st World Library Literary Society is a nonprofit organization dedicated to promoting literacy by:

- Creating a free internet library accessible from any computer worldwide.
- Hosting writing competitions and offering book publishing scholarships.

The Path of Life

contributed by Tim, Ed & Rodney

in support of

1st World Library Literary Society

CONTENTS

TRANSLATOR'S NOTE

In introducing this new writer to the English-speaking public, I may be permitted to give a few particulars of himself and his life. Stijn Streuvels is accepted not only in Belgium, but also in Holland as the most distinguished Low-Dutch author of our time: his vogue, in fact, is even greater in the North Netherlands than in the southern kingdom. And I will go further and say that I know no greater living writer of imaginative prose in any land or any language. His medium is the West-Flemish dialect, which is spoken by perhaps a million people inhabiting the stretch of country that forms the province of West Flanders and is comprised within the irregular triangle outlined by the North Sea on the west, the French frontier of Flanders on the south and a line drawn at one-third of the distance between Bruges and Ghent on the east. In addition to Bruges and Ostend, this province of West Flanders includes such towns as Poperinghe, Ypres and Courtrai; and so subtly subdivided is the West-Flemish dialect that there are words which a man of Bruges will use to a man of Poperinghe and not be understood.

It is one of the most interesting dialects known to me, containing numbers of mighty mediaeval words which survive in daily use; and it is one of the richest: rich especially - and this is not usual in dialects - in words expressive of human characteristics and of physical sensations.

Thus there is a word to describe a man who is not so much a poor wretch, *un miserable*, as what Tom Hood loved to call "a hapless wight:" one who is poor and wretched and outcast and out of work, not through any fault of his own, through idleness or fecklessness, but through sheer ill-luck. There is a word to describe what we feel when we hear the tearing of silk or the ripping of calico, a word expressing that sense of angry irritation which gives a man a gnawing in the muscles of the arms, a word that tells what we really feel in our hair when we pretend that it "stands on end." It is a sturdy, manly dialect, moreover, spoken by a fine, up-standing race of "chaps," "fellows," "mates," "wives," and "women-persons," for your Fleming rarely talks of "men" or "women." It is also a very beautiful dialect, having many words that possess a charm all their own. Thus *monkelen*, the West-Flemish for the verb "to smile," is prettier and has an archer sound than its Dutch equivalent, *glimlachen*. And it is a dialect of sufficient importance to boast a special dictionary (*Westvlaamsch Idiotikon*, by the Rev. L. L. De Bo. Bruges, 1873) of 1,488 small-quarto pages, set in double column.

In translating Streuvels' sketches, I have given a close rendering: to use a homely phrase, their flavour is very near the knuckle; and I have been anxious to lose no more of it than must inevitably be lost through the mere act of translation. I hope that I may be forgiven for one or two phrases, which, though not existing, so far as I am aware, in any country or district where the English tongue is spoken, are not entirely foreign to the genius of that tongue. Here and there, but only where necessary, I have added an explanatory foot-note.

For those interested in such matters, I may say that Stijn Streuvels' real name is Frank Lateur. He is a nephew of Guido Gezelle, the poet-priest, whose statue graces the public square at Courtrai, unless indeed by this time those shining apostles of civilization, the Germans, have destroyed it. Until ten years ago, when he began to come into his own, he lived at Avelghem, in the south-east corner of West Flanders, hard by Courtrai and the River Lys, and there baked bread for the peasant-fellows and peasant-wives. For you must know that this foremost writer of the Netherlands was once a baker and stood daily at sunrise, bare-chested, before his glowing oven, drawing bread for the folk of his village. The stories and sketches in the present volume all belong to that period.

Of their number, *Christmas Night*, *A Pipe or no Pipe*, *On Sundays* and *The End* have appeared in the *Fortnightly Review*, which was the first to give Stijn Streuvels the hospitality of its pages; *In Early Winter* and *White Life* in the *English Review*; *The White Sand-path* in the *Illustrated London News*; *An Accident in Everyman*; and *Loafing* in the *Lady's Realm*. The remainder are now printed in English for the first time.

ALEXANDER TEIXEIRA DE MATTOS.

Chelsea, *April*, 1915.

I

THE WHITE SAND-PATH

I was a devil of a scapegrace in my time. No tree was too high for me, no water too deep; and, when there was mischief going, I was the ring-leader of the band. Father racked his head for days together to find a punishment that I should remember; but it was all no good: he wore out three or four birch-rods on my back; his hands pained him merely from hitting my hard head; and bread and water was a welcome change to me from the everyday monotony of potatoes and bread-and-butter. After a sound drubbing followed by half a day's fasting, I felt more like laughing than like crying; and, in half a while, all was forgotten and my wickedness began afresh and worse than ever.

One summer's evening, I came home in fine fettle. I and ten of my school-fellows had played truant: we had gone to pick apples in the priest's orchard; and we had pulled the burgomaster's calf into the brook to teach it to swim, but the banks were too high and the beast was drowned. Father, who had heard of these happenings, laid hold of me in a rage and gave me a furious trouncing with a poker, after which, instead of turning me into the road, as his custom was, he caught me up fair and square, carried me to the loft, flung me down on the floor and bolted the trap-door behind him.

In the loft! Heavenly goodness, in the loft!

Of an evening I never dared think of the place; and in bright sunshine I went there but seldom and then always in fear.

I lay as dead, pinched my eyes to and pondered on my wretched plight. 'Twas silent all around; I heard nothing, nothing. That lasted pretty long, till I began to feel that the boards were so hard and that my body, which had been thrashed black and blue, was hurting me. My back was stiff and my arms and legs grew cold. And yet I nor wished nor meant to stir: that was settled in my head. In the end, it became unbearable: I drew in my right leg, shifted my arm and carefully opened my eyes. 'Twas so ghastly, oh, so frightfully dark and warm: I could see the warm darkness; so funny, that steep, slanting tiled roof, crossed by black rafters, beams and laths, and all that space beyond, which disappeared in the dark ridgework: 'twas like a deserted, haunted booth at a fair, during the night. Over my head, like threatening blunderbusses, old trousers and jackets hung swinging, with empty arms and legs: they looked just like fellows that had been hanged! And it grew darker, steadily darker.

My eyes stood fixed and I heard my breath come and go. I pondered how 'twould end here. That lasting silence affrighted me; the anxious waiting for that coming night: to have to spend a long, long night here alone! My hair itched and pricked on my head. And the rats! I gave a great loud scream. It rang in anguish through the sloping vault of the loft. I listened as it died away ... and nothing followed. I screamed again and again and went on, till my throat was torn.

The gruesome thought of those rats and of that long night drove me mad with fear. I rolled about on the floor, I struck out with my arms and legs, like one possessed, in violent, childish fury. Then, worn out, I let my arms and legs rest; at last, tired, swallowed up in my helplessness, left without will or feeling, I waited for what was to come. I had terribly wicked thoughts: of escaping from the house, of setting fire to the house, of *murder*! I was an outcast, I was being tortured. I should have liked to show them what I could do, who I was; to see them hunting for me and crying; and then to run away, always farther away, and never come back again.

Downstairs, the plates and forks were clattering for supper. I was not hungry; I did not wish nor mean to eat. I heard soft, quiet voices talking: that made me desperate; they were not speaking of me! They had no thought nor care for the miscreant; they would liefst have him dead, out of the way. And I was in the loft!

Later, very much later, I heard my little brother's voice saying evening prayers - I would not pray - and then I heard nothing more, nothing; and I lay there, upstairs, lonely and forlorn....

I walked all alone in the forest, through the brushwood. 'Twas half-dark below; but, above the bushes, the sun was playing as through a green curtain. I went on and on. The bushes here grew thick now and the tiny path was lost. After long creeping and stumbling, I leapt across a ditch and entered the wide drove. It did not seem strange to me that 'twas even darker here and that the light, instead of from above, came streaming low down from between the trunks of the trees. The vault was closed leaf-tight and the trunks hung down from out of it like pillars. 'Twas silent all around. I went, as I thought that I must see the sun, round behind the trunks, half anxious at last to get out of that magic forest; but new trees kept coming up, as though out of the ground, and hid the sun. I would have liked to run, but felt I know not what in my legs that made me drag myself on.

Far beyond, on the road-side grass, sat two boys. It was ... but no, they were sitting there too glumly! I went up to them and, after all, knew them for Sarelke and Lowietje, the village-constable's children. They sat with their legs in the ditch, their elbows on their knees, earnestly chatting. I sat down beside them, but they did not even look up, did not notice me. Those two boys, my schoolmates, the worst two scamps in the village, sat there like two worn-out old fogies: they did not know me. This ought to have surprised me, and yet I thought that it must be right and that it had always been so. They chatted most calmly of the price of marbles, of the way to tell the best hoops, of buying a new box of tin soldiers; and they mumbled their words as slowly as the priest in his pulpit. I became uncomfortable, felt ill at ease in that stifling air, under that half-dusk of the twilight, where everything was happening so earnestly, so very slowly and so heavily. I, who was all for sport and child's-play, now found my own chums so altered; and they no longer knew me. I would have liked to shout, to grip them hard by the shoulder and call out that it was I: I, I, I! But I durst not, or could not.

"There - comes - the - keeper," droned Sarelke.

Lowietje looked down the drove with his great glassy eyes. The two boys stood up and, without speaking, shuffled away. I saw them get smaller and smaller, till they became two black, hovering little specks that vanished round the bend.

I was alone again! Alone, with all those trees, in that frightful silence all around me. And the keeper, where was he? He would come, I knew it; and I felt afraid of the awful fellow. I must get away from this, I must hide myself. I lay down, very slowly, deep in the ditch. I now felt that I had been long, long dead and that I was lying here alone, waiting for I forget what. That keeper: was there such a person? He now seemed to me an awesome clod of earth, which came rolling down, slowly but steadily, and which would fall heavily upon me. Then he turned into a lovely white ashplant, which stood there waving its boughs in a stately manner. I would let him go past and then would go away. People were waiting for me, I had to be somewhere: I tried mightily to remember where, but could not.

The keeper did not come.

The ditch was cold, the bottom was of smooth, worn stone and very hard. I lay there with gleaming eyes: above my head stood the giant oaks, silently, and their knotted branches ran up and were lost in the dark sky.

The keeper came, I heard his coming; and the wind blew fearfully through the trees. I shivered....

I woke with fright and I was still lying in my loft. The hard bottom of the ditch was the boarded floor and the tree-trunks were the legs of father's trousers and the branches ran up and were lost in the darksome roofwork. Two sharp rays of light beamed through the shut dormer-window. It must be day then! And this awful night was past! All my dismay was gone and a bold feeling came over me, something like the feeling of gladness that follows on a solved problem. I would make Lowietje and Sarelke and all the boys at school hark to my tale, that I would! I had slept a whole night alone in the loft! And the rats! And the ghosts! Ooh! And not a whit afraid!

I got up, but that was such a slow business. I still felt that dream and that slackness in my limbs. I was so stiff; that heavy gloom, that slow passing of time still lingered - just as in my dream - in my slow breathing. I still saw that forest and, shut up as I was, with not a single touchstone for my thoughts, I began to doubt if my dream was done and I had to feel the trouser-legs to make sure that they were not really trees.

Time stood still and there was no getting out of my mind the strange things seen in that dream-forest, with those earnest, sluggish, elderly children and that queer keeper. 'Twas as though some one were holding my arms and legs tight to make them move heavily, deadly heavily; and I felt myself, within my head, grown quite thirty years older, become suddenly an old man. I walked about the loft; I wanted to make myself heard, but my footsteps gave no sound.

I grew awfully hungry. Near the ladder-door, I found my prison fare. I nibbled greedily at my crust of bread and took a good drink of water.

I now felt better, but this doing nothing wearied me; I became sad and felt sorry to be sitting alone. If things had gone their usual gait, I should now be with my mates at school or playing somewhere under the open sky; and that open sky now first revealed all its delightfulness. The usual gait, when all was said, was by far the best.... All alone like this, up here.... Should I go down and beg father's pardon? Then 'twould all be over and done with....

"No!" said something inside me, "I stay here!"

And I stayed.

I shoved a box under the dormer-window, I pushed open the wooden shutter ... and there! Before me lay the wide stretch in the blazing sunlight! My eyes were quite blind with it.

'Twas good up here and funny to see everything from so high up, so endlessly far! And the people were no bigger than tiny tadpoles!

Just under my dormer-window came a path, a white sand-path winding from behind the house and then running forwards to the horizon in a line straight as an arrow. It looked like a naked strip of ground, powdered white and showing up sharply, like a flat snake, in the middle of the green fields which, broken into their many-coloured squares, lay blinking in the sun.

This path was deserted, lonely, as though nor man nor beast had ever trodden it. It lay very near the house and I did not know it from up here; it looked now like a long strip of drab linen, which lay bleaching in a boundless meadow. And that again suited my lonely-ness so well! At last, I looked and saw nothing more. And that path!...

Slowly, overcome by that silent, restful idleness, I fell

a-dreaming; and that path, that long, white path seemed to me to have become a part of my own being, something like a life that began over there, far away yonder in the clear blue, to end in the unknown, here, behind the gable-end, cut off at that fatal bend.

After long looking, I saw something, very far off; it came so slowly, so softly, like a thing that grows, and those two little black patches grew into two romping schoolboys, who, rolling and leaping along, came running down the white sand-path and, at last, disappeared in the bend behind the gable-end.

Then, for another long while, nothing more, nothing but sand, green and sunshine.

Later, 'twas three labourers, who came stepping up briskly, with their gear over their shoulders. Half-way up the path, they jumped across the ditch and went to work in the field. They toiled on, without looking up or round, toiled on till I got tired of watching and tired of those three stooping men and of seeing that gleaming steel flicker in the sun and go in and out of the earth.

When now 'twas mid-day and fiercely hot in my loft, my three labourers sat down behind a tree and ate their noonday meal.

I went to the loft-door and devoured my second crust of bread and took a fresh gulp of water.

Very calmly, without thinking, lame with the heat and with that old-man's feeling still inside me, I went and sat at the window.

The three men worked on, always, without stopping.

And that went on, went on, until the evening! When 'twas nearly dark, they gathered up their tools, jumped over the ditch, walked down the path the way they had come and disappeared behind the gable-end.

Now it became deadly.

In the distance appeared a great black patch, which came slowly nearer and nearer. The patch turned into a lazy, slow-stepping ox, with a jolting, creaking waggon, in which sat a little old man who gazed stupidly in front of him into the dark distance. The cart dragged along wearily, creeping through the sand, and first the ox, then the little fellow, then the waggon disappeared behind the gable-end.

Now I felt something like fear and I shivered: the evening was coming so slowly, so sadly; and I dared not think of the night that was to follow. 'Twas the first time in my life that I fell earnestly a-thinking. So that path there became a life, a long-drawn-out, earnest life.... That was quite plain in my head; and those boys had rolled and tumbled along that path; next, those big men had burdensomely, most burdensomely turned over their bit of earth; and the ox and the little old fellow had joggled along it so piteously.... That life was so earnest and I had seen it all from so far, from the outside of it: I did nothing, I took no part in it and yet I lived ... and must also one day go along that path!

And how?

Getting up in the morning, eating, playing, going to school, misbehaving, playing, eating, sleeping....

The mist rose out of the fields and I saw nothing more.

I jumped off my box, begged father's pardon and crept into bed.

Never again was I shut up in the loft.

II

IN EARLY WINTER

First the leaves had become pale, deathly pale; later they turned yellow-brown; and then they went fluttering and flickering, so wearily, so slackly, like the wings of dying birds; and, one after the other, they began to fall, dancing gently downwards, in eddies. They whirled in the air, were carried on by the wind and at last fell dead and settled somewhere in the mud.

Not a living thing was to be seen and the cottages that sat huddled close to the ground remained fast shut; the smoke from the chimneys alone still gave a sign of life.

The green drove now stood bare and bleak: two rows of straight trunks which grew less and faded away in the blue mist.

Yonder comes something creeping up: a shapeless thing, like two little black stripes, with something else; and it approaches....

At last and at length, out of those little stripes, appear a man and a wife; and, out of the other thing, a barrel-organ on a cart, with a dog between the wheels.

It all looked the worse for wear. The little fellow went

bent between the shafts and tugged; the little old woman's lean arms pushed against the organ-case; and the wheeled thing jolted on like that over the cart-ruts, along the drove and through the wide gate of an honest homestead.

A flight of black crows sailed across the sky. The wind soughed through the naked tree-tops; the mist rose and the world thinned away in a bluey haze; this all vanished and slowly it became dark black night.

Man, woman and dog, they crept, all three, high into the loft and deep into the hay; and they dozed away, like all else outside them and around. Warm they lay there! And dream they did, of the cold, of the dark and of the sad moaning wind!

At early morning, before it was bright day, they were on the tramp, over the fallow fields, and drowned in a huge sea of thick blue mist. They pulled for all they could: the little fellow in the shafts, the little old woman behind the cart and the dog, with his head to the ground, for the road's sake.

A red glow broke in the east and a new day brightened. 'Twas all white, snow-white, as if the blue mist had bleached, melted and stuck fast on the black fields, on the half-withered autumn fruits and on the dark fretwork of the trees. Great drops dripped from the boughs.

From under the peak of his cap, the fellow peered into the distance with his one eye, and he saw a church and houses. They went that way.

'Twas low-roofed cottages they saw, all covered with

hoar-frost; here and there stood one alone and then a whole little row, crowded close together: a street.

They were in the village.

It was lone and still, like a cloister, with here a little woman who, tucked into her hooded cloak, crept along the houses to the church; there a smith who hammered ... and the little church-bell, which tinkled over the house-tops.

They stopped. The dog sat down to look. The little fellow threw off his shoulder-strap, pulled his cap down lower and felt under the red-brown organ-cloth for the handle. He gave a look at the houses that stood before him, pinched his sunken mouth, wiped the seam of his sleeve over his face and started grinding. Half-numbed sounds came trickling into the chill street from under the organ-cloth: a sad - once, perhaps, dance-provoking - tune, which now, false, dragging and twisted out of shape, was like a muddled crawling of sounds all jumbled up together; some came too soon, the others too late, as in a weariful dream; and, in between, a sighing and creaking which came from very deep down, at each third or fourth turn, and was deadened again at once in those ever-recurring rough organ-sounds or dragged on and deafened in a mad dance. 'Twas like a poor little huddled soul uttering its plaint amid the hullabaloo of rude men shouting aloud in the street.

The dog also had begun to howl when the tune started.

The little wife had settled her kerchief above her sharp-featured old-wife's face; and, with one hand in her apron-pocket and the other holding a little tin can, she now went from door to door:

"For the poor blind man.... God reward you."

And this through the whole street and farther, to the farmhouses, from the one to the other, all day long, till evening fell again and that same thick mist came to wrap everything in its grey, dark breath.

And again they wandered, through a drove, to a homestead and into the hay.

"The dog has pupped," said the little old woman; and she shook her man.

"Pupped?..."

And he turned in the nest which he had made for himself, pushed his head deeper in the hay and drowsed on. He dreamt of dogs and of pups and of organs and of ear-splitting yelps and howls.

The dog lay in a fine, round little nest of his own, rolled into a ball and moaning. And he[1] looked so sadly and kindly into the little old woman's eyes; and he licked, never stopped licking his puppies. They were like three red-brown moles, each with a fat head; they wriggled their thick little bodies together and sought about and squeaked.

[1] The West-Fleming talks of dogs of either sex invariably as "he."

When the tramps had swallowed their slice of rye-bread and their dish of porridge, they went on, elsewhither. The little fellow tugged, the little old woman pushed and the dogs hung swinging between the wheels, in a fig-basket. So they went begging, from hamlet to hamlet, the wide world through: an old man and woman, with their organ; and a dog with his three young pups.

* * * * *

Much later....

The thick mist had changed into bright, glittering dewdrops and the sun shone high in the heaven. Now four dogs lay harnessed to the cart, four red-brown dogs. And, when the handle turned and the organ played, all those four dogs lifted their noses on high and howled uglily.

Inside, deep-hidden under the organ-cloth, sat the little soul, the mysterious, shabby little organ-soul, grown quite hoarse now and almost dumb.

* * * * *

III

CHRISTMAS NIGHT

Over there, high up among the pines, stood the house where he lived alone with the trees and the birds; and there, every morning, he saw the sun rise and, in the evening, sink away again. And for how many years!

In summer, the white clouds floated high over his head; the blackbirds sang in the wood around his door; and before him, in a blue vista, lay the whole world.

When his harvest was gathered and the days drew in, when the sky closed up, when the dry pines shook and rocked in the sad wind and the crows dropped like black flakes and came cawing over the fields, he closed his windows and sat down in the dark to brood.

He must go down yonder now, to the village below.

He fetched his Christmas star from the loft, restuck the gold flowers and paper strips and fastened them in the cleft of the long wand. Then he put on his greatcoat, drew the hood over his head and went.

From behind the black clouds came a light, a dull copper glow, without rays, high up where the stars were; it set golden edges to the hem of the clouds; the heaven remained black. There appeared a little streak of glowing copper, which grew and grew, became a sickle, a half-disk and at last a great, round, giant gold moon, which rose and rose. It went up like a huge round orange behind the heaven and, more and more swiftly, shot up into the sky, growing smaller and smaller, till it became just a common moon, the laughing moon among the stars.

He alone had seen it.

Now he took his star on his shoulder, pulled his hood deep over his head and wandered down the little path, all over the snow, to where the lights were burning. It was lonely, lifeless, that white plain under that burnished sky; and he was all alone, the black fellow on the snow. And he saw the world so big, so monotonously bleak; a flat, white wilderness, with here and there a straight, thin poplar and a row of black, lean, knotty willows.

He went down towards the lights.

The village lay still. The street was black with people. Great crowds of womenfolk, tucked and muffled in black hooded cloaks, tramped as in a dream along the houses, over the squeaking snow. They shuffled from door to door, stuck out their bony hands and asked plaintively for their God's-penny. They disappeared at the end of the street and went trudging into the endless moonlight.

Children went with lights and stars and stood gathered in groups, their black faces glowing in the shine of their lanterns; they made a huge din with their tooting-horns[2] and rumble-pot[3] and sang of

The Babe born in the straw

and

The shepherds they come here.
They're bringing wood and fire
And this and that and t'other:
Now bring us a pot of beer.

[2] A cow's horn fitted with a mouthpiece.

[3] An iron pot with a bladder stretched across the top, beaten with sticks, like a drum.

Mad Wanne went alone; she kept on lurching across the street with her long legs, which stuck out far from under her skirt, and held her arms wide open under her hooded cloak, like a demon bat. She snuffled something about:

'Twas hailing, 'twas snowing and 'twas bad weather
And over the roofs the wind it flew.
Saint Joseph said to Mary Maid:
"Mary, what shall we do?"

Top[4] Dras, Wulf and Grendel, three fellows, tall as trees, were also loafing round. They were the three Kings: Top had turned his big jacket and blackened his face; Grendel wore a white sheet over his back and blew the horn; and Wulf had a mitre on and carried a great star with a lantern on a stick. So they dragged along the street, singing at every door:

Three Kings with a star
Came travelling from afar,
Over mountains, hills and dale,

To go and look
In every nook,
To go and look for the Lord of All.

[4] Beggar.

Their rough voices droned and three great shadows walked far ahead of them on the white street-snow. All those people came and went and twisted and turned and came and went again. Each sang his own little song and fretted his whining prayer. Above all this rose the dull toot of the baker's horn, as he kept on shouting:

"Hot bread! Hot bread!"

High hung the moon and blinked the stars; and fine white shafts fell through the air, upon everything around, like silver pollen.

"Maarten of the mountain!" whispered the children behind the window. "Maarten the Freezyman!"[5]

[5] A legendary figure of a snow-covered bogie, who comes down to the villages at Christmas-time and runs away with the children.

And they crept back into the kitchen, beside the fire.

And the black man stood outside the door, tugging at the string of his twirling star, and sang through his nose:

Come, star, come, star, you must not so still stand!
You must go with me to Bethlehem Land,
To Bethlehem, that comely city,

Where Mary sits with her Babe on her knee....

Along the country-roads, the farmhouses stood snowed in, with black window-shutters, which showed dark against the walls and shut in the light, and stumpy chimneys, with thick smoke curling from them. Indoors, there was no seeing clearly: the lamp hung from the ceiling in a ring of steam and smoke and everything lay black and tumbled. In the hearth, the yule-log lay blazing. The farmer's wife baked waffles and threw them in batches on the straw-covered floor.

In one corner, under the light and wound from head to foot in tobacco-smoke, were the farm-hands, playing cards. They sat wrapped up in their game, bending over their little table, very quiet. Now and then came a half-oath and the thud of a fist on the table and then again peaceful shuffling and stacking and playing of their cards.

The Freezyman sat in the midst of the children, who listened open-mouthed to his tale of *The Mighty Hunter*.

His star stood in the corner.

Later, the big table was drawn out and supper served. All gathered round and sat down and ate. First came potatoes and pork, red kale and pigs' chaps, then stewed apples and sausages ... and waffles, waffles, waffles. They drank beer out of little glass mugs. The table was cleared, coffee poured out, spirits fetched from the cupboard and gin burnt with sugar. Then the chairs were pushed close, right round the hearth, and Maarten stood up, took his star, smoothed his long beard and, keeping time by tugging the string of his star, droned out:

On Christmas night
Is Jesus born
To fight our fight
Against the night
Of Satan and his devil-spawn.
And a manger is His cot
And all humble is His lot;
So, mortal, make you humble, too,
To serve Him Who thus served you.

Three wise men and each a king
Come to make Him offering;
Gold, frankincense and myrrh they bring.
Angels sweet
Kiss His feet,
As they sing:
"Hail, Lord and King!"
Telling all mankind the story
Of His wonder and His glory;
So, mortal, make you humble, too,
To serve Him Who thus served you.

All else was still. The men sat drinking their hot gin, the children listened with their heads on one side and the farmer's wife, with her hands folded over her great lap, sat crying.

The door opened and the Kings stood in the middle of the floor. They were white with snow and their faces blue with cold; the ice hung from Grendel's moustache. They looked hard under their hats at the table, the hearth and the little glasses and at Maarten, who was still standing up. Wulf made his star turn, Top banged his rumble-pot to time and they sang:

Three Kings came out of the East;
'Twas to comfort Mary....

When the song was ended, each got two little glasses; then they could go.

Grendel cursed aloud.

"That damned hill-devil swallows it all up," muttered Wulf.

And they went off through the snow.

The others sang and played and played cards for ever so long and 'twas late when Maarten took his star and, with a "Good-night till next year," pulled the door behind him.

It was still light outside, but the sky hung full of snow; above, a grey fleece and, lower, a swirl of great white flakes, which fell down slowly swarming one on top of the other.

He plunged deep into it.... It was still so far to go; and his house and his pines, he had left them all so far behind.

He was so old, so lone; it was so cold; and all the roads were white ... all sky and snow. In the hollow lay the village: a little group of sleeping houses round the white church-steeple; and behind it lay his mountain, but it was like a cloud, a shapeless monster, very far away.

Above his head, stars, stars in long rows. He stood still and looked up and found one which he saw every evening, a pale, dead star, like an old acquaintance, which would lead him - for the last time, perhaps - back to his mountain, back home.

And he trudged on.

There was a light in the three narrow pointed windows of the chapel and the bell tinkled within. He went to rest a bit against the wall. What a noise and what a bustle all the evening ... and the gin! And those rough chaps had looked at him so brutally. In there, it was still; those windows gleamed so brightly; and, after the sound of the bell, there came so softly a woman's voice:

"*Venite adoremus....*"

Then all was silence, the lights went out. And he fared on.

The village lay behind him and the road began to climb. There, on the right, stood "The Jolly Hangman." Now he knows his way and 'tis no longer far from home. From out of the ditch comes something creeping, a black shape that runs across the plain, chattering like a magpie: Mad Wanne, with her thin legs and her cloak wide open. She ran as fast as she could run and vanished behind the inn.

He had started; he became so frightened, so uneasy, that he hastened his steps and longed to be at home.

There was still a light in "The Jolly Hangman" and a noise of drunken men. He passed, but then turned back again ... to sing his last song, according to old custom. They opened the door and asked him in. He saw

Grendel sitting there and tried to get away. Then the three of them rushed out and called after him. When they saw that he went on, they broke into a run:

"Stop, you brute!... Here, you with your star!... Oh, you damned singer of songs!" they howled and ran and caught him and threw him down.

Grendel dug his knee into his chest and held his arms stretched wide against the ground. Wulf and Dras gripped whole handfuls of snow and crammed it into his mouth and went on until all his face was thickly covered and he lay powerless. Then they planted his star beside him in the snow and began to turn and sing to the echo:

> *A, a, a* - glory be to Him on high to-day!
> *E, e, e* - upon earth peace there shall be!
> *I, i, i* - come and see with your own eye!
> *O, o, o* - His little bed of straw below!

Like a flash, Mad Wanne shot past, yelling and shrieking. Wulf flung his tick against her legs. She waved her arms under her cloak and vanished n the dark.

The three men sat down by the ditch and laughed full-throated. Then they tarted for the village. Long it rang:

> Three Kings came out of the East;
> 'Twas to comfort Mary ...

Great white flakes fell from the starry sky, wriggled and swarmed, one on op of the other.

IV

LOAFING

He went, ever on the move, with the slow, shuffling step of wandering beggars who are nowhere at home.

They had discharged him, some time ago, and now he was walking alone like a wild man. For whole days he had dragged himself through the moorland, from farm to farm, looking for his bread like the dogs. Now he came to a wide lane of lime-trees and before him lay the town, asleep. He went into it. The streets lay dead, the doors were shut, the windows closed: all the people were resting; and he loafed. It was dreary, to walk alone like that, all over the country-side, and with such a body: a giant with huge legs and arms, which were doomed to do nothing, and that belly, that craving belly, which he carried about with him wherever he went.

And nobody wanted him: 'twas as though they were afraid of his strong limbs and his stubborn head - because his glowing eyes could not entreat meekly enough - and his blackguardly togs....

Morning came; the working-folk were early astir. Lean men and pale women, carrying their kettles and food-satchels in their hands, beat the slippery pavements with their wooden shoes. Doors and windows flew open; life began; every one walked with a busy air, knew where he was going; and they vanished here and there, through a big gate or behind a narrow door that shut with a bang. Carts with green stuff, waggons with sand and coal drove this way and that. Fellows with milk and bread went round; and it grew to a din of calls and cries, each shouting his loudest.

And he loafed. Nobody looked at him, noticed him or wanted him. In the middle of the forenoon, a young lady had stared at him for a long time and said to her mother:

"What a huge fellow!"

He had heard her and it did him good. He looked round, but mother and daughter were gone, behind a corner, and stood gazing into a shop full of bows and ribbons.

It began to whirl terribly in his belly; and his stomach hurt him so; and his legs were tired.

The streets and houses and all those strange people annoyed him. He wanted to get away, far away, and to see men like himself: workers without work, who were hungry!

He looked for the narrow alleys and the poor quarter.

Out of a side-street a draycart came jogging along. Half a score of labourers lay tugging in the shoulder-strap or leant with all the force of their bodies against the cart, which rolled on toilsomely. 'Twas a load of flax, packed tightly in great square bales standing one against the other, the whole cart full. The dray caught its right wheel in the grating of an open gutter and remained stock-still, leaning aslant, as though planted there. The workmen racked and wrung to get the wheel out, but it was no good. Then they stood there, staring at one another, at their wits' end and throwing glances into the eyes of that big fellow who had come to look on. Without saying or speaking, he caught a spoke in either hand, pressed with his mighty shoulder against the inside of the wheel, bent and wrung and in a turn brought the cart on the level. Then he went behind among the other workmen to go and help them shove. They looked at him queerly, as if to say that they no longer needed his help and had rather done without him. The cart rolled on, another street or two, and then through the open gate of the warehouse. The labourers looked into one another's eyes uneasily, moved about, pulled the bales off the cart and dragged them a little farther along the wall. Then they tailed off, one by one, through a small inner door; and he stood there alone, like a fool. A bit later, he heard them laugh and whisper under their breaths. When he was tired of waiting, he went up the street again.

Nobody, nobody, nobody wanted him!

He ground his teeth and clenched his fists. In the street through which he had to go, on the spaces outside the hotels sat ladies and gentlemen toying with strange foods and sipping their wine out of long goblets. They chattered gaily and tasted and pecked with dainty lips and turned-up noses. The waiters ran here, there, like slaves. Those coaxing smells stung like adders and roused evil thoughts in his brain. His stomach fretted awfully and his empty head turned.

He hurried away.

In a street with windowless house-fronts, a street without people in it, he felt better. He let his body lean against the iron post of a gas-lamp, stuck his hands in his trouser-pockets and stood there looking at the paving-stones. Now he was damned if he would take another step, he would rather croak here like a beast; then they would have to take him up and know that he existed.

The boys coming from school mocked him; they danced in a ring, with him, the big fellow, in the middle. They hung paper flags on his back and sang:

> Hat, hat,
> Ugly old hat!
> It serves as a slop-pail and as a hat!

He did not stir.

Yon came a milk-maid driving up in a cart drawn by dogs. He got a gnawing in his arms, a spout of blood shot to his head and he suddenly felt as if something was going to happen. Just as she drove past, he put his great hand on the edge of the little cart, with one pull took a copper can from its straw, put it to his mouth and drank; then he sent the can clattering through the window of the first-best house, till the panes rattled again. Looking round - as if bewildered and set going, roused by what he had done - he caught sight of the frightened little dairy-maid. A mocking grin played on his cruel face; he flung his rough arm round her little body and lifted the girl out of the cart right up to his face in a fierce hug.

The boys had fled shrieking. He felt two pairs of hands pulling at his sleeves from below. He loosed the girl and saw two policemen who held him fast and ordered him to go with them. They held him by the arm on either side and stepped hurriedly to keep pace with his great strides. They looked in dismay at that huge fellow, with his wicked eyes, and then at each other, as if to ask what they should do.

They came to a narrow little street, with nobody in it, and stopped at a public-house:

"Could you do with a dram, mate?" they asked him.

He looked bewildered, astounded. They all three went inside; and each of them drank a big glass of gin.

The policemen whispered something together; the elder wiped the drink from his moustache and then said, very severely:

"And now, clear out; hurry up! And mind your manners, will you, next time!"

He was outside once more, loafing on, along the houses.

V

SPRING

Mother stood like a clucking hen among her red-cheeked youngsters. She was holding a loaf against her fat stomach and, with a curved pruning-knife, was cutting off good thick slices which the youngsters snatched away one by one and stuffed into their pockets. Horieneke fetched her basket of knitting and her school-books. She first pulled Fonske's stocking up once more, buttoned Sarelke's breeches and wiped Lowietje's nose; and, with an admonishing "Straight to school, do you hear, boys?" from mother, the whole band rushed out of the door, through the little flower-garden and up the broad unmetalled road, straight towards the great golden sun which was rising yonder, far behind the pollard alders, in a mighty fire of rays. It was cool outside; the sky was bright blue streaked with glowing shafts aslant the hazy-white clouds deep, deep in the heavens. Over the level fields, ever so far, lay a stain of pale green and brown; and the slender stalks of the wheat stood like needles, quivering in their glittering moisture. The trees were still nearly bare; and their trunks and tops stood tall and black against the clear sky; but, when you saw them together, in rows or little clusters, there was a soft yellow-green colour over them, spotted with gleaming buds ready to burst. A soft wind, just warm enough to thaw the frost, worked its way into and through everything and made it all shake and swarm till it was twisted full of restless, growing life. That wind curled through the youngsters' tangled hair and coloured their round cheeks cherry-red. They ran and romped through the dry sand, stamping till it flew above their heads. They were mad with enjoyment.

Trientje stood in the doorway, in her little shirt, with her stomach sticking out, watching her brothers as they disappeared; and, when she saw them no longer, she thrust her fists into her sockets, opened her mouth wide and started a-crying, until mother's hands lifted her up by the arms and mother's thick lips gave her a hearty kiss.

Horieneke came walking step by step under the lime-trees, along the narrow grass-path beside the sand, keeping her eyes fixed on the play of her knitting-needles. When she reached the bridge that crossed the brook, she looked round after her brothers. They had run down the slope and were now trotting wildly one after the other through the rich brown grass, pulling up all the white and yellow flowers, one by one, till their arms were crammed with them. Horieneke took out her catechism, laid it open on the low rail and sat there cheerfully waiting. Sarelke had crept through the water-flags until he was close to the brook and, through the clear, gleaming blue water, watched a little fish frisking about. In a moment, his wooden shoes and his stockings were off and one leg was in the water, trying it: it was cold; and he felt a shiver right down his back. Ripples played on the smooth blue and widened out to the bank. The little fish was gone, but so was the cold; and he saw more fish, farther away: quick now, the other leg in the water! He pulled his breeches up high and there he stood, with the water well above his knees, peering out for fish. The water was clear as glass; and he saw swarms of them playing, darting swiftly up and down, to and fro like arrows: they shot past in shoals that held together like long snakes, in among the moss and the reeds and between the stones, winding through slits and crannies. He shouted aloud for joy. Bertje and Wartje and the others all had their stockings off and stood in the water bending down to look, making funnels of their hands in the water, where it rustled in little streams between two grass-sods through which the fish had to pass. Whenever they felt one wriggling in their hands they yelled and screamed and sprang out of the brook to put it into their wooden shoes, which stood on the bank, scooped full of water. There they loitered examining those beasties from close by: those fish were theirs now; and they would let them swim about in the big tub at home and give them a bit of their bread and butter every day, so that they might grow into great big pike. And now back to the runnel for more.

"Boys, I'll tell mother!" cried Horieneke.

But they did not hear and just kept on as before. Fonske had not been able to catch one yet and his fat legs were turning blue with the cold. In front of him stood Bertje, stooping and peering into the water, with his hands ready to grasp; and Fonske saw such a lovely little runnel from his neck to halfway down his back, all bare skin. He carefully scooped his hands full of water and let it trickle gently inside Bertje's shirt. The boy growled; and Fonske, screaming with laughter, skipped out of the brook. Now came a romping and stamping in the water, a dashing and splashing with their hands till it turned to a rain of gleaming drops that fell on their heads and wetted their clothes through and through. And a bawling! And a plashing with their bare legs till the spray spouted high over the bank.

"The constable!" cried Horieneke.

The sport was over. Like lightning they all sprang out of the brook, caught up their wooden shoes with the little fish in them and ran as hard as they could through the grass to the bridge. There only did they venture to look round. Hurriedly they turned down their breeches, dried their shiny cheeks and dripping hair with one another's handkerchiefs and then marched all together through the sun and wind to school.

In the village square they wandered about among the other boys, silently showed their catch, hid their shoes in the hawthorn-hedge behind the churchyard and stayed playing until schoolmaster's bell rang.

Boys and girls, each on their own side, disappeared through the gate; and the street was now silent as the grave. After a while, there came through the open window of the school first a sort of buzzing and humming and then a repetition in chorus, a rhythmical spelling aloud: b-u-t, but; t-e-r, ter: butter; B-a, Ba; b-e-l, bel: Babel; ever on and more and more noisily. In between it all, the sparrows chattered and chirped and fluttered safely in the powdery sand of the playground.

The sun was now high in the sky and the light glittered on the young leaves, full of the glad life of youth and gleaming with gold.

Horieneke, with a few more children, was in another school. They sat, the boys on one side and the girls on the other, on long benches and were wrapped up in studying their communion-book and listening to an old nun, who explained it to them in drawling, snuffling tones. After that, they had to say their lesson, one by one; and this all went so quietly, so modestly, so easily, 'twas as if they had the open book before them. Half-way through the morning, they went two and two through the village to the church, where the priest was waiting to hear their catechism. This also went quietly; and the questions and answers sounded hollow in that empty church.

Horieneke sat at the head of the girls; she had caught up almost half of them because she always knew her lessons so well and listened so attentively. She was allowed to lead the prayers and was the first examined; then she sat looking at the priest and listening to what came from his lips. He always gave her a kind smile and held her up to the others as an example of good conduct. After the catechism, they had leave to go and play in the convent-garden. In the afternoon, there were new lessons to be learnt and new explanations; and then quietly home.

So they lived quite secluded, alone, in their own little world of modesty and piety, preparing for the great day. The other youngsters, who went their several ways, felt a certain awe for these school-fellows who once used to romp and fight with them and who were now so good, so earnest, so neat in their clothes and so polite. The "first-communicants:" the word had something sacred about it which they respected; and the little ones counted on their fingers how many years they would have to wait before they too were learning their catechism and having leave to play in the convent-garden.

To her brothers Horieneke had now become a sacred thing, like a guardian angel who watched over them everywhere; and they dared do no mischief when she was by. She no longer played with them after school; she was now their "big sister," to whom they softly whispered the favours which they wished to get out of mother.

When Trientje saw her sister coming home in the distance, she put out her little arms and then would not let her go. For mother, Horieneke had to wash the dishes, darn the stockings and, when the baby cried, sit for hours rocking it in the cradle or dandling it on her lap, like a little young mother.

Holding Trientje by the hand and carrying the other on her arm, she would walk along the paths of the garden and then put them both down on the bench in the box arbour, while she tended the plants and shrubs that were beginning to shoot.

In the evening, when the bell rang for benediction, she called all her little brothers and they went off to church together. From every side came wives in hooded cloaks and lads in wooden shoes that stamped on the great floor till it echoed in the silent nave.

The choir was a semicircular, homely little chapel, with narrow pointed windows, black at this hour, like deep holes, with leads outlining saints in shapeless dark patches of colour. The altar was a mass of burning candles; and a flickering gleam fell on the brass candlesticks, the little gold leaves and the artificial flowers and on the corners of the silver monstrance, which stood glittering high up in a little white satin house. All of this was clouded in a blue smoke which rose from the holes of the censer continuously swung to and fro by the arm of a roguish serving-boy. Far at the back, in the dark, in the black stripes of shadow cast by the pillars or under the cold bright patch of a lamp or a stand of votive candles was an old wife, huddled under her hood, with bent back, praying, and here and there a troop of boys who by turns dropped their wooden shoes or fought with one another's rosaries.

Near the communion-bench knelt Horieneke, her eyes wide open, full of brightness and gladness and ecstacy, face to face with Our Lord. The incense smelt so good and the whole little church was filled with the trailing chords of the organ and with soft, plaintive Latin chant. Her lips muttered automatically and the beads glided through her fingers: numbered Hail Marys like so many roses that were to adorn her heart against the coming of the great God. Her thoughts wafted her up to Heaven in that wide temple full of glittering lights where, against the high walls full of pedestals and niches, the saints, all stiff with gold and jewels, stood smiling under their haloes and the nimble angels flew all around on their white-plaster wings. She had something to ask of every one of them and they received her prayer in turns. When the priest stood up in his gleaming silver cope, climbed the three steps and took the Blessed Sacrament in his white hands to give the benediction; when the bell tinkled and the censer flew on high and the organ opened all its throats and the glittering monstrance slowly made a cross in the air and above the heads of the worshippers, she fell forward over her praying-stool and lay like that, swooning in mute adoration, until all was silent again, the candles out and she sitting alone there in the dark with a few black shapes of cloaked women who wandered discreetly from one station of the Cross to the next. Outside she heard her brothers playing in the church-square. There she joined the little girls of her school; and, arm in arm, they walked along past the dark houses and the silent trees, each whispering her own tale: about her new dress, her veil, her white shoes, her long taper with golden bows; about flowers and beads and prayers....

After supper, Horieneke had to rock the baby to sleep, while mother moved about, and then to say the evening prayers out loud, after which they all of them went to bed. On reaching her little bedroom, she visited all the prints and images hanging on the walls. She then undressed and listened whether any one was still awake or up. Next she carefully crept down the three stairs[6] in her little shift and clambered up the ladder to the loft, where all her little brothers lay playing in a great box-bed. They knew that she would come and had kept a place for her in the middle. She sank deep in the straw and, when they all lay still, she went on with the tale which she had broken off yesterday half-way. It was all made up of long, long stories out of *The Golden Legend* and wonderful adventures of far beyond the sea in unknown lands. She told it all so prettily, so leisurely; and the children listened like eager little birds. High up in the dusk of the rafters they saw all those things happening before their eyes in the black depths and saw the mad fairy-dance there, until they dreamed off for good and all and Horieneke was left the only one awake, still telling her story. Then she crept carefully back to her room and into bed, where she lay counting: how many more days, how many times sleeping and getting up and how many more lessons to learn ... and then the great day! The great day! Slowly she made all the days, with their special happenings, appear before her eyes; and she enjoyed beforehand all those beautiful things which had kept her so long a-longing. When, in her thoughts, it came to Saturday evening and at last, slowly - like a box with something wonderful inside which you daren't open - to that Sunday morning, then her heart began to flutter, a thrill ran through her body and, so that she shouldn't weep for gladness, she bit her lips, squeezed her hands between her knees and rubbed them until the ecstasy was passed and she again lay smiling in supreme content and shivering with delight.

[6] The bedroom behind the kitchen or living-room, in the Flemish cottages, is over the cellar; but this cellar is not entirely underground and is lighted by a very low window at the back. Consequently, the floor of the bedroom is a little higher than that of the living-room and is approached by a flight of two or three steps.

Time dragged on; cold weather came and rain and it seemed as if it never would be summer. And that constant repetition of getting up and going to bed and learning her lessons and counting the hours and the minutes became so dreary and seemed to go round and round in an endless circle.

To-day at last was the long-awaited holiday when Horieneke might go into town with mother to buy clothes. Her heart throbbed; and she walked beside mother, with eyes wide-open, looking round at every window, up one street and down another, crying aloud each time for joy when she saw pretty things displayed. They bought white slippers with little bows, a splendid wreath of white lilies of the valley, a great veil of woven lace, a white-ivory prayer-book, a mother-of-pearl rosary with a little glass peep-hole in the silver crucifix, showing all manner of pretty things. Horieneke sighed with happiness. Mother haggled and bargained, said within herself that it was "foolishness to waste all that money," but bought and went on buying; and, every time something new went into the big basket, it was:

"Don't tell father what it cost, Rieneke!"

All those pretty things were locked away in the bedroom at home and hung up in the oak press, while father was still at work.

On another evening, when mother and Horieneke were alone at home, the seamstress brought the new clothes: a whole load of white muslin in stiff white folds full of satin bows and ribbons and white lace. They had to be tried on; and Horieneke stood there, for the first time in her life, all in white, like an angel. But the happiness lasted only for a spell: there came a noise and every one in the room fled and the clothes were hastily taken off and put away.

Every day, when the boys were at school and father in the fields, neighbours came to look at the clothes. Piece after piece was carefully taken out of the press and spread out for show on the great bed. The wives felt and tested the material, examined the tucks and seams and the knots and the lining, the bows and ribbons and clapped their hands together in admiration. It became known all over the village that Horieneke would be the finest of all in the church.

The counted days crept slowly by, the sun climbed higher every day and the mornings and evenings lengthened. Things out of doors changed and grew as you looked: the young green stood twinkling on every hand; the fields lay like coloured carpets, sharply outlined; and the trees grew long, pale branches with leaves which stood out like stately plumes against the sky, so full of youth and freshness and free from dust as yet and tender. In course of time, white buds came peeping, gleaming amid the delicate young leaves, till all looked like a spotted altar-cloth: a promising splendour of white blossoms. Here and there in the garden an early flower came creeping out. Yonder, in the dark-blue wood, patches of brown and of pale colour stood out clearly, with a whole variety of vivid hues. And it had all come so unexpectedly, all of a sudden, as though, by some magic of the night, it was all set forth to adorn and grace a great festival.

In the fields, the folk were hard at work. The land was turned up and torn and broken by the gleaming plough and lay steaming in purple clods in the sun's life-giving rays. Everything swarmed with life and movement. The houses were done up and coated with fresh whitewash, the shutters painted green, till it all shouted from afar in a glad mosaic, with the blue of the sky and the young leafage of the trees, under the brown, moss-grown roofs.

And the days crept on, each counted and marked off: so many white stripes on the rafters and black stripes on the almanack; they fell away one by one and the Saturday came, the long-expected eve of the great Sunday. Quite early, before sunrise, the linen hung outside, the white smocks and shirts waving, like fluttering pennons, from the clothes-lines in the white orchard. Horieneke also was up betimes and helping mother in her work. From top to bottom everything had to be altered and done over again and cleansed. It was only with difficulty that she got to school. The last time! To-day, the great examination of conscience, the general confession and the communion-practice; and, to-night, everything to be laid out ready for to-morrow morning: all this kept running anyhow through her head and among the lines of her lesson-book.

Half-way through the morning they went to church. The children there all looked so glad, so happy and so clean and neat in their second-best clothes and so nicely washed. They now made their confessions for the last time; and it all went so pleasantly: they had done no wrong for such a long while and all their sins had already been forgiven two or three times over, yesterday and the day before. They sat in two long rows waiting their turns and thinking over, right away back to their far-off babyhood, whether nothing had been forgotten or omitted: their little hearts must be quite stainless now and pure. When they were tired of examining their consciences, they fell to praying, with their eyes fixed upon the saint who stood before them on his pedestal, or else watched the other youngsters going in and out by turns.

The little church looked its best, neat as a new pin: the floor was freshly scrubbed and the chairs placed side by side in straight rows; the brasswork shone like gold; and a new communion-cloth hung, like a snow-white barrier, in front of the sanctuary. The velvet banners were stripped of their linen covers; and the blue vases, with bright flowers and silver bunches of grapes, were put out on the altar, as on feast-days. And all of this was for to-morrow! And for them!

All the time it was deathly still, with not a sound but that of the youngsters going in and out of the creaking confessional. Now and then the church-door flapped open and banged to, when one of the children had finished and went away. Their little souls were white as new-fallen snow and bedight with indulgences and prayers. On their faces lay the fresh innocence of babes brought to baptism or of laughing angels' heads and in their wide eyes everything was reflected festively and at its best; they felt so light and lived on little but longing and a holy fear of their own worthiness: that great, incredible thing of the morrow was suddenly going to change them from children into grown-up people!

They just gave themselves time to have their dinners in a hurry; and then back to school, where they were to learn how to receive communion. A few benches placed next to one another represented the communion-rails; and there they practised the whole afternoon: with studied piety, their hands folded and their heads bowed, they learnt how to genuflect, how to rise, how to approach in ranks and return at a sign from the old nun, who tapped with a key on the arm of her chair each time that a new row of youngsters had to start, kneel or go back. In a short time this went as exactly, as evenly as could be, just like soldiers drilling. Finally, they had to recite once more their acts of faith, adoration and thanksgiving; and Horieneke and the first of the little boys had to write out on large sheets of paper the preparation and thanks which they had learnt by heart, to be read to-morrow in church. After that, they were drawn up in line and silently and mysteriously led into the convent.

The children held their breath and walked carefully down long passages, between high, white walls, past closed doors with inscriptions in Gothic letters and a smell of clean linen and apples: ever on and on, through more passages, till they reached a large hall full of chairs where Mother Prioress - a fat and stately nun, with her great big head covered by her cap and her hands in her sleeves - sat upon a throne. They had to file past her, one by one, with a low bow, and then sit down.

Mother Prioress settled herself in her seat, coughed and, in a rich, throaty voice, began by telling the youngsters how they were to address Our Lord; told stories of children who had become saints; and she ended by slowly and cautiously producing a little glass case in which a thorn out of Our Lord's crown lay exposed on a red-velvet cushion. And then they were sent home.

On the way, Horieneke came upon her brothers playing in the sand. They had scooped it up in their wooden shoes and poured it into a heap in the middle of the road and then wetted it; and now they were boring all sorts of holes in it and tunnels and passages and making it into a rats'-castle. She let them be, gathered up her little skirts, so as not to dirty them, and passed by on one side.

Mother was up to her elbows in the golden dough of the cakebread, stirring and beating and patting the jumble of eggs and flour and milk. Horieneke took the crying baby out of the cradle, shaking and tossing it in the air, and went into the garden just outside the door. The golden afternoon sun lay all around and everything was radiant with translucid green. The little path lay neatly raked and the yellow daffodils stood, like brass trumpets, closely ranked on their stalks; under the shrubs bright violets peeped out with raised eyebrows, like the grinning faces of little old wives. The whole garden was filled with a scent of fresh jasmine and a cool fragrance of cherry-blossom and peach.

It was all so still and peaceful that Horieneke, who had begun to sing, stopped in the middle and stood listening to the chaffinches and siskins chattering pell-mell.

From there she went to her little bedroom, laid the child on her bed and drew the curtains before the window which let in the sun in a thousand slender beams of dusty light. The pictures and images gleamed on the wall and the saints seemed to smile with happiness in that cool air, fragrant of gillyflowers and white jasmine. She took out her new prayer-book, flicked the silver clasp open and shut and played with the little shaft of light which the gilt edge sent running all round the white walls. Then she stood musing for a long time, gazing out through the little curtains at those white trees in blossom, around and above which the golden pollen danced, and at all that huge green field and the everlasting sun and all the blue on the horizon. And, feeling tired, she laid her head on the bed beside the baby and lingered there, dreaming of all the delight and beauty of the morrow.

Mother called her and Horieneke came down. Mam'selle Julie was there, who had promised to come and curl the child's hair. Mam'selle put on a great apron and began to undress Horieneke; then a great tub of rain-water was carried in and the girl was scrubbed and washed with scented soap till the whole tub was full of suds. Her head was washed as well and her hair plaited into little braids, which were rolled up one by one and wound in curl-papers and fastened to her head, under a net. Her cheeks and neck shone like transparent china with the rosy blood coursing underneath. When she was done, Mam'selle Julie went off to the other communicants.

The boys were lying on their backs, under the walnut-tree, talking, when Horieneke came past. They looked at the funny twists on her head and went on talking: Wartje longed most of all to put on his new breeches; Fonske was glad that Uncle Petrus was coming to-morrow and Aunt Stanske and Cousin Isidoor; Bertje because of the dog-cart[7] and the dogs and the chance of a ride; Wartje because of all that aunt would bring with her in her great wicker basket; and Dolfke longed for father to come home from work, so that he might help to clean the rabbits.

[7] The Flemish low-wheeled cart drawn by dogs.

The sun played with the gold in the leaves of the walnut-tree; and the radiant tree-top was all aswarm and astir and little golden shafts were shooting in all directions. The first butterfly of the year rocked like a white flower through the air.

"I smell something!" said Dolfke.

They all sniffed and:

"Mates! They're taking the cake-bread out of the oven!"

They rushed indoors one on top of the other. On the table lay four golden-yellow brown-crusted loaves, as big as cart-wheels, steaming till the whole house smelt of them.

"First let it cool! Then you can eat it," said mother and gave each of them a flat scone.

"Yes, mother."

And they trotted round the kitchen holding their treasures high above their heads and screaming with delight.

Behind the elder-hedge they heard father's voice humming:

> When the sorrel shows,
> 'Tis then the month of May, O!...

They ran to him, took the tools out of his hands and:

"Father, the rabbits! The rabbits now, father?"

"Will it be fine weather to-morrow?" asked Horieneke.

"For sure, child: just see how clear the sun is setting."

He pointed to the west; and the boys stood on tip-toe to see the sinking, dull-glowing disk hang glittering in its gulf of orange cloud-reefs, pierced through and through with bright rays that melted away high in the pale blue and grey, while that disk hung there so calmly, as though frozen into the sky for ever.

Father had one or two things to do and then the boys might come along to the rabbits.

"The two white ones, eh, father?"

Father nodded yes; and Sarelke and Dolfke skipped along the boards to the hutch and came back each carrying a long white rabbit by the ears.

Dolfke held his close to the ground, hidden behind a tree, so that it shouldn't see the other's blood and foresee its own death. While father was sharpening his knife, Fonske took a cord and tied the hind-legs of Sarelke's rabbit and hung it, head down, on a nail under the eaves. Father struck it behind the ears so that it was dazed and, rolling its eyes, remained hanging stock-still. Before it had time to scream, the knife was in its neck and the throat was cut open. A little stream of dark blood trickled to the ground and clotted; and some of it hung like an icicle from the beard, which dripped incessantly with red drops.

Fonske carefully put his finger to the rabbit's nose and licked off a drop of blood.

"It's going home," said Sarelke.

"Is it dead, father?" sighed Wartje.

"Stone-dead, my boy."

He ripped one buttock with his knife and pulled off the skin; then the other, so that the blue flesh was laid bare and the little purple veins. One more tug and the creature hung disfigured beyond all knowledge, in its bare buttocks and its fat, bulging paunch, with its head all over blood and its eyes sticking out. The belly and breast were cut open from end to end and the guts removed; the gall-bladder was flung into the cess-pool; two bits of stick, to keep the hind-legs and the skin of the stomach apart, and the thing was done. The other was treated likewise; and the two rabbits hung skinned and cleaned, stiffening high up on the gable-end.

Meanwhile mother had got supper ready: a heap of steaming potatoes soaking in melted butter and, after that, bread-and-butter and a pan of porridge. Horieneke, by way of a treat, got a couple of eggs and a slice of the new cakebread; and she sat enjoying this at the small table. After supper, the boys had to be washed and cleaned. They started undressing here and undressing there; serge breeches and jackets flew over the floor; and one after the other they were taken in hand by mother, beside a kettle of water, where they were rubbed and rinsed with foaming soap-suds. Then each was given a clean shirt; and away to bed with them! They jumped and, with their shirt-tails waving behind them, skipped about and smacked one another until father came along and stopped their game. Mother had still her floor to scrub; and Horieneke read out evening prayers while the boys knelt beside their bed.

Now all grew still. Father smoked a pipe and took a stroll in the moonlight through the orchard, where he had always something to look after or to do. Indoors the broom went steadily over the floor; whole kettlefuls of water were poured out and swept away and rubbed dry. Then the stove was lit; and, while mother blacked the shoes, father made the coffee. They mumbled a bit together - about to-morrow's doings, about the children, the work, the hard times and their troublesome landlord, the farmer of the woodside - when there came a noise from the little bedroom and the door creaked softly. Horieneke suddenly appeared in the middle of the floor in her little nightgown; and, before father and mother had got over their surprise, the child was on her knees, asking:

"Forgive me, father and mother, for all the wrong that I have done you in my life; and I promise you now to be always good and obedient...."

Mother was furious at first; and then, at the sight of the kneeling figure and the sound of the tearful little voice, her anger fell and she felt like crying. Father hated all that sentimental rubbish:

"Come, you baggage, quick to bed!... Forgive you? What for?... Nonsense, nonsense!"

The child kept on weeping:

"Father, please, it's my first communion to-morrow and we must first receive forgiveness: Sister at school said so...."

"The sisters at school are mad! And they'll make you mad too! To bed with you now, d'you hear?"

Mother could stand it no longer; she sobbed aloud, took Horieneke under the arms and lifted her to her breast. She felt a lump in her throat and could hardly get out her words:

"It's all forgiven, my darling. God bless you and keep you! And now go quick to bed; you have to be up early to-morrow."

Horieneke put her arm over mother's shoulders and whispered softly in her ear:

"I have something else to ask you, mother. All the

children's parents are going to communion to-morrow: shall you too, mother?"

"Make your heart easy, dear; it'll be all right."

"Mother, will you call me in good time to-morrow morning?"

"Yes, yes; go to bed."

The house grew quiet as the grave; and soon a manifold snoring and grunting sounded all through the bedroom and the loft. Outside it was twilight and the blossoms shone pale white in the orchard. The crickets chirped far and near....

This was the last evening and morning: when it was once more so late and dark, everything would be over and done! All those days, all that long array of light and darkness, of learning and repeating lessons - a good time nevertheless - was past and gone; and, now that the great thing, always so remote, so inaccessible, was close at hand, she was almost sorry that the longing and the aching were to cease and she almost felt afraid. Should she dare to sleep to-night? No. 'Twas so good to lie awake thinking; and she had still so much praying to do: her heart was still far from ready and prepared.

"O God, I am a poor little child and Thou art willing to come to me.... Dear Virgin Mary, make my soul as pure as snow, so that it may become a worthy dwelling-place for thy Divine Son."

The white dress now lay spread out upon the best bed in the big bedroom and her wreath too, with all the rest. She already saw herself clad in all that white wealth like a little queen, standing laughing through her golden curls! She felt the little knots of paper on her head; to-morrow they would be released and would open into a cloud of ringlets; and the people, who would all look at her; and aunt.... Now just to recite her words once more for to-morrow in church.... And that pretty picture which the priest would give her.... Was she sure that nothing was forgotten? Just let her think again: and her candle-cloth? Yes, that was there too.... What could the time be? The clock was ticking like a heavy chap's footstep downstairs in the kitchen. It was deathly quiet everywhere. Now she would lie and wait until the clock struck, so that she might know how long it would be before it grew light. Her eyes were so tired and all sorts of things were walking higgledy-piggledy up the white wall....

Then, in the solemn stillness, the nightingale began to sing. Three clear notes rang out from the echoing coppice; it was like the voice of the organ in a great church. It sounded over the fields, to die away in a low, hushed fluting. Now, louder and staccato, like a spiral stair of metallic sound, the notes rang out, high and low alternately, in quickening time, a running, rustling and rioting, with long-drawn pipings, wonderfully sweet, that rose in a storm of bell-like tinklings, limpid as water, with a strength, a violence, a precision exceeding the music of a hundred thousand tipsy carrillons pealing through the silent night. And now again the notes were softly weaving their fabric of sound: bewitchingly quiet, intimately sweet, musingly careful, like the music of tiny glass bells; and once more they were louder and again they fainted away, borne on the still wind like the murmur of angels praying.

The blue velvety canopy was stretched on high, studded with twinkling stars; and all about the country-side the trees stood white. On the winding paths, among the pinks, anemones, guelder-roses and jasmine-bushes, walked stately white figures in trailing garments, with wreaths of white roses and yellow flowers gleaming on their golden tresses, which they shook out over their white shoulders. All the world was one pure vista full of blue, curling mist and fresh, untasted fragrance. A soft melody of dreamy song was wafted through the air. And Horieneke saw herself also playing in that great garden, an angel among angels. Ropes hung stretched from tree to tree; and they swung upon them and rocked with streaming hair and fluttering garments, floating high above the tree-tops, light as the wind, in a shower of white blossoms. They sang all together, with those who lay on the beds of white lilies and violets: a song of unheard sweetness. Not one spoke of leaving off or going home; they only wished to stay like that, without rain or darkness; there was a continual happy frolic, a glad gaiety, in those spacious halls where, in spite of the singing and the music, all things were yet so deliciously, languidly still, still as the moonlight.

Yonder, by the dark wood, the steady swish of a sickle was heard; and this made a fearsome noise in the tenuous night. A gigantic man stood there; his head looked over the trees and his wide-stretched arms swung the sickle and a pick-hook; and, stroke by stroke, the foliage and the flowers fell beneath his hands as he passed. The singing gradually ceased, the swings fell slack and the frolic changed into an anxious waiting, as before thunder. One and all stood in terror and dismay staring at that giant approaching. The blue of the sky darkened and the angels vanished, like lamps that were blown out. The flowers were faded and the whole plain lay mown flat, like a stricken wilderness; and that fellow with his sickle, who now drew himself up to contemplate his finished work, was ... her father!

She started awake and trembled with fright. It had been so beautiful that she sighed at the thought of it; and outside was the twilight of advancing dawn. It was daylight! Sunday! She jumped out of bed in a flash and pulled open the window. The trees were there still and the flowers too and all the white of last night, but so pale, dim and colourless beside the glittering brightness of a moment ago ... and never an angel! She gave a sigh. The sky was hung with a thick grey shroud; and in the east a long thin cleft had been torn in the grey; and behind that, deep down, was a dull-golden glow, gleaming like a great brazen serpent. A keen wind shook the cherry-blossom and blew a cold, fragrant air into the window. All the green distance lay dead as yet, half-hidden, asleep in the morning mist; and neither man nor beast was visible, nor even a wreath of smoke from a chimney.

What was the time? She threw a wrap over her shoulders, which were getting chilled, and went carefully down the bedroom steps. It was still dark in the kitchen. She groped, found and lit a sulphur match and lifted the flame to the clock. Four! She was so much used to seeing the hands in that position in the afternoon and they now looked so silly that she stood for a long time thinking, foolishly, what she ought to do: call mother or creep back into bed and sleep. She felt so uncomfortably cold and it was still so dark: she went up again and stood looking out.

The birds twittered in the trees and the wide cleft in the east yawned wider and wider. Was it going to be a fine day after all? Everything for which she had waited so long was there now and so strange, so totally different from what she had imagined: instead of that leaping gladness there was something like fear and nervous trembling; she could have wept; and, merely for the sake of doing something, she went down on her knees beside the bed and said the prayers which she had learnt by heart:

"Lord God, I give Thee my heart. Deign to make Thyself a worthy dwelling in it and to abide there all the days of my life...."

The clock struck; it was half-past four and no one yet astir.

Now she went downstairs again. In the room lay her white dress, her wreath, her prayer-book: it was all ready; if only somebody would wake! Dared she call? They lay sleeping side by side: father was snoring, with his mouth open, and mother's fat stomach and breasts rose and fell steadily.

"Mother!"

Nobody heard.

"Mother!!"

And then she pulled at the coverlet and cried repeatedly, a little louder each time:

"Mother! Mother!! Mother!!!"

That was better. Mother turned on her side, lifted her head and rubbed her eyes with her hands.

"Mother, it's nearly five; we shall be late!"

Mother, drunk with sleep, kept on looking at the window and yawning:

"Yes, child, I'll come at once."

She got up and came out in her short blue petticoat stretched round her fat hips, with an open slit behind, and her loose jacket and wooden shoes on. She lit the stove. Horieneke read her morning prayers. Mother's heavy shoes clattered over the floor outside and in again; she put on and took off the iron pots with the goats' food, drew fresh water and made the coffee.

Mam'selle Julie was coming along the rough road.

"You're in good time!" cried mother from the doorway.

"Good-morning, Frazie. Up already, Horieneke? It'll be a fine day to-day."

She took off her hooded cloak, put on a clean apron and turned up her sleeves. Horieneke was washed all over again while mother poured out the coffee. Then they sat down. Horieneke kept her lips tight-closed so as not to forget that she must remain fasting. She slowly pulled on her new stockings and stretched out her hand to the bench on which the white slippers lay. She took off her sleeping-jacket and her little skirt and stood waiting in her shift. When the tongs were well warmed, Mam'selle Julie seized the little paper twists in the hot iron and opened them out. From each fold a curled tress came rolling down; and at last, combed out and bound up with blue-silk ribbon, it all stood about her head in a light mist of pale-gold silk, like a wreath of light around her bright, fresh face. Her dirty shift was dragged off downwards and mother fetched the new scapular and laid it over the child's bare shoulders. The first-communion chemise was of fine white linen and trimmed with crochet lace. Julie took out the folds and drew it over Horieneke's head. Then came white petticoats, bodices and skirts. The child stood passively, in the middle of the floor, with her arms wide apart to give free room to Julie, who crept round on her knees, sticking in a pin here, smoothing a crease there. Mother fetched the things as they were wanted. There was a constant discussing, approving, asking if it wouldn't meet or if it hung too wide, all in a whisper, so as not to wake the boys.

There came a scrabbling overhead and down the stairs; and, before any one suspected it, Bertje stood dancing round Horieneke in his shirt.

"Jesu-Maria! Oo, you rascal!"

And the corset which mother held in her hand was sent flying up the stairs after the boy, who in three jumps was gone and up above. The others lay laughing in bed when Bertje told them that he had seen Horieneke all in white, with a bunch of red-gold curls round her head, and that mother had thrown something at him.

The corset was laced up and Mam'selle Julie told the child to hold her breath to let them get her body tighter. Now for the white frock: the skirt was slipped down over her head until it stood out in light, stiff pleats; the white bodice encased her body firmly and stuck out above the shoulders, its puffed sleeves trimmed with little white-satin bows and ribbons at every seam and fold. Over it hung the veil, which shrouded her as in a white cloud. The wreath was put on, looked at from a distance and put on again until it was right at last, with the glittering beads in front, shining among the auburn curls, and the long streamer of threaded lilies of the valley behind, nestling in the tresses on her back. The white gloves, her prayer-book and candle-cloth, a few pennies in her bead purse; and 'twas done.

The child was constantly twisted and turned and examined from every side. She did not know herself in all her splendour: the Horieneke of yesterday, in her blue bird's-eye bib and black frock was a poor thing compared with the present Horieneke, something far removed from this white apparition, something quite forgotten. She stood stiff as a post in the middle of the kitchen, without daring to look round or stir; she felt so light and airy in those rustling folds and pleats and all that muslin that she seemed not to touch the ground. She did not know what to do with her arms, how to tread with her feet; and her thoughts were straying: the part she had to play was all gone out of her head; she would be as fine as this all day long, but oh, so uncomfortable!

Mother put on stockings and shoes, donned her cap, turned her apron, threw her cloak over her shoulders; she called her husband; then:

"There, boys, we're off; don't forget your drop of holy water, all of you!"

The door fell back into the latch with a bang; and the

three of them were on the road. A gust of wind laden with white blossoms out of the orchard greeted them. Horieneke held the tips of her veil closed against the wind and stepped out like a little maid in a procession. The two women came behind and had no eyes for anything but Horieneke: the fall of those white folds, the whirling of the veil and the dancing of the lilies of the valley in the auburn locks. They said nothing.

The sky still hung grey with its yawning cleft widening in the east; and out of it there beamed a sober, uncertain light, which fell upon everything with a dead gleam: it was like noonday in winter. Over the fields and in the trees drifted thin wisps of mist, like floating blue veils blown on by the wind. Below in the meadow the cock had started crowing amid his flock of peacefully pecking pullets. It was very fresh, rather cold indeed, out on the high road.

All the little paths led to the church; and in every direction, along the flat fields, came people in their very best, with little white maids. The wind played in their white veils and set them waving and flapping like wet flags.

"The children'll have good weather," said Mam'selle Julie; and, a little later, to Horieneke, "What are you going to ask of Our Lord now, dear?"

"Oh, so much, so much, Mam'selle Julie! I myself hardly know.... For father and mother and all the family and that I may always be a good girl and stay at home with them and not fall among wicked people and that we may all live a long time and go to Heaven...."

"And that the harvest may succeed and we be able to

pay the rent ... and for the farmer ... and that father may keep in health and be fit to work," mother ordered.

They reached the village. Mother remained waiting among the folk in the street; Horieneke, with the other youngsters, went through the school-gates where their wax tapers stood burning above the bunches of gold flowers and leaves shining in the warm light. The children looked at one another's clothes, whispered in one another's ears what theirs had cost and wrangled as to which looked the prettiest. The boys vied with one another in showing their bright pennies and their steel watch-chains.

The procession filed out: first the acolytes, in scarlet, with gleaming crucifix, brass candle-sticks and censer, followed by boys and girls symbolically dressed, a lilting dance of flags and banners in brilliant colours. Next came the priest, in a gorgeous vestment stiff with silk and silver thread and gold tracery; and, in two rows, on either side of the street, preceded by four little angels with gold wings, the first-communicants, really such on this occasion, in their proper clothes, with the great wax tapers in their white-gloved hands and a glow in their faces and laughter in their eyes. All the people crowded after them, through the street to the church. The bells rang out, the priest sang with the sacristan and the whole procession triumphantly entered the wide church-doors. There was a mighty stamping and pushing to get near and to see the children sitting in straight rows on the front benches of the nave. The girls settled in their clothes and the boys looked down at their stiff, wide cloth breeches and their new shoes, or shoved their fingers up their noses or into their tight collar-bands. The organ droned out a mighty prelude; the priest, all in gold, stood at the altar; the ceremony began; the people were silent and prayed over their prayer-books.

The sun appeared! And green and red and yellow shafts of light slanted through the stained-glass panes and mingled with the blue incense-wreaths. They made the corners of the brasswork shine and brought smiles to the faces of the saints in their niches. A splash of gold fell on the curly heads of the children, dark and fair; and tiny rays flashed upon the gilt edges of their prayer-books. The congregation prayed diligently and the full voices sang the joyful *Gloria in excelsis* with the organ.

After the Gospel, the priest hung up his chasuble on the stand and mounted the pulpit. After a noisy shifting of chairs and dragging of feet and coughing, the people sat still, with their faces turned to the priest. He began by reading out the notices in a snuffling tone: the intentions of the masses for the ensuing week; the names of those about to be married or lately deceased. Then he waited, cast his eyes over that level multitude of raised heads, pulled up his white sleeves and turned his face towards the children. His drawling voice wished them *proficiat*.

It was the first time in their lives that the youngsters saw that face turned expressly towards them from a pulpit and also the first time that they listened to the sermon with attention. They kept their eyes fixed on the priest so as not to lose a word. The great day had arrived; a few moments more and they would be completing the solemn task, they, small children, the task that was denied to the pure angels in heaven.

"And that work must be the foundation on which all your future life is based. Your souls are now so clean, so pure, they are shining like clear water and are quite spotless. For years we have taught and instructed and prepared you in order to teach your virgin hearts, this day, now, in this beautiful chapel, to receive that strengthening food, that miracle of God's love. Remember it always: this is the happiest day of your lives! You are still innocent and about to receive the Bread that raises the dead, cleanses sinners and purifies the fallen. You are still in your first youth, without experience of life, and are already allowed to approach the Holy Table and share the strengthening food that supports men and women in the trials of life. This also is the propitious moment, the mighty hour in which Our Lord can refuse you nothing that you ask Him. So make use of it, ask Him much, ask Him everything: for your parents and your masters, who have done so much for you, for your pastors, your village and especially for yourselves, that He may keep you from sin and continue to dwell in your hearts and allow you to grow up into stout champions of the faith and of your religion. It is the happiest day of your lives. You are here now, to-day, with your bright, clear eyes, young and beautiful as angels; we have watched over you, sheltered you against all that could have harmed or offended your innocence, far from the corrupt world of whose existence you have not even known. But to-morrow you will enter the wide world, with only your weak flesh to fight against life's dangers: depravity, falsehood, lies and sin. Now life will begin for you, now for the first time will you be called upon to fight, to show courage and to stand firm. How many of those who once sat where you are now sitting and who were pure and innocent as yourselves have now, alas, become lost sinners, Judases who have rejected their

God, devils as roaring lions going about seeking whom they may devour! Be strong, listen to your good parents: it is to them alone that you will have to listen henceforth...."

He turned round to the other side and, continuing with the same rise and fall in his voice, the same gestures of his thin right arm, with the flowing white sleeve, and the same movement of his sharp profile high up above the congregation, he began once more:

"To you, fathers and mothers, I also wish a cordial *proficiat*; for you also this is a glad and memorable day. How long is it not since you were kneeling there! And yet that day always lingers in your memory. Since that time you have been plunged into the world, have had to struggle and have perhaps fallen and more than once have known your courage fail you. Now your children are sitting there! For years you have left them to our care and to-day we give them back to you, instructed, enriched and supplied with all that they can need to pass onward. You receive them this day from our hands pure and innocent as on the day of their baptism. It is for you henceforth to preserve and to maintain that virtue and purity in them; it is for you to bring up these children so that later they may be exemplary Christians. See to it that your own conduct edifies them: it is according to you and all your actions that they will order their lives and take example. Admonish them in good season and chastise them when necessary: 'He that spareth the rod hateth his son,' says the Holy Ghost. And keep your eyes open, for God will ask an account of your stewardship and will reward or punish you according as you have brought them up well or ill. A good son, a virtuous daughter are the joy and the comfort of their parents."

The congregation were greatly impressed. The mothers wept: the priest was such a good, worthy old man, whom they had known all their lives; and they liked hearing him say all those beautiful things: that reference to their own childhood and to their youngsters, whom they now saw sitting there so good and saintlike, waiting to receive Our Lord, brought the tears to their eyes; and it did them good to feel their hearts throb, to feel that lump in their throats; and they let the tears flow: after all, it was from gladness.

The organ played softly and the changing tones mingled with the blue wreaths that ascended from the sanctuary in a fragrant cloud, lingering over the congregation. The celebrant offered the bread and wine to Our Father in Heaven. And all this took time; the children were tired by their tense concentration; their prayers had all been said two and three times over; and they were now vacantly waiting and longing, looking at their clothes, at the stained-glass windows in the choir or St. Anne in her crimson cloak, or counting the stars that were painted high up on the stone ceiling.

The altar-bell tinkled twice and thrice in succession, the *Sanctus* was sung; and after that the organ was silenced. A hush fell over the congregation and all heads dropped, as though mown down, in deep reverence: not one dared look up. The priest genuflected, the bell sounded repeatedly and, amid that great hush, thrice three notes of the great church-bell droned through the church and rang out over the distant fields. Outside, it was all blue and sunshine and silence; everything was bowed in anxious expectation; it was as though there were nothing erect and alive in the world except that little church and that bell. In the farthest houses in the village the mothers were now kneeling and beating their breasts, with their thoughts on Our Lord. The God of Heaven and Earth had descended and was filling all things with His awful presence. Carefully, slowly, almost timidly came the *Adoro te*; and the people little by little raised their heads and sighed, as though relieved and still quite awed by what had happened or was going to happen.

And now the ceremony began. After the *Agnus Dei* and the three tinkles of the bell at the *Domine, non sum dignus*, the four little angels came with hands folded and heads bowed, with their gold-paper wings carefully furled behind them, and walked reverently to the front of the church. Horieneke stood up, took her great sheet of paper and, in her clear voice, read out her piece so that all the congregation could hear, though she stopped to find her words at times and faltered here and there because her heart was beating so violently and she had such a catch in her throat:

"Then Thou wilt come to us, Almighty God! To us poor little sheep who, hardly knowing what we did, have so often offended Thee. We are not worthy to receive Thee, unless Thou say but the word that our souls may be healed. And, as Thou hast ordained, we will, in fear and confidence, approach Thee as poor little children approaching their kind Father. We have nothing wherewith to repay the great love which Thou bearest us; we are needy in all things; and all things must come from Thee. We are still very young and have already gone astray, but we repent and are heartily sorry to have caused Thee any grief. And, now that Thou art so unspeakably good to us, we wish to be wholly loyal to Thee and to belong to Thee with heart and soul; dispose of us henceforth as Thy servants and we shall be filled with joy. Come then, O Jesus; our hearts pant with longing, our souls are now prepared; we have begged Mary, our dear Mother, our guardian angels and our blessed patron saints to make us worthy habitations for Thy majesty."

The silence was so great that one could hear a leaf fall. The congregation wriggled where they knelt to see and held their breaths, full of expectation. The nun struck her key on the back of her chair. Two little angels went, step by step, to the communion-bench and the first row of boys and girls followed. The little ones now looked very serious. They held their heads bowed and their hands clasped; and their faces shone with heavenly light and silent inner happiness. Horieneke was now like a white flower; her transparent little waxen face, her delicately chiselled nose and closed pink lips looked so angelic under her sunny curls and the white of her veil. The children approached the choir silently and slowly: 'twas as though they were floating. At the second tap of the key, they knelt; one more ... and their hands were under the lace communion-cloth. From the organ-loft the *Magnificat* resounded. The priest took the ciborium, gave the benediction and with stately tread descended the altar-steps. In his slender fingers he held the Sacred Host, that small white disk which stood out sharply above the silver vessel against the rich violet of his chasuble. The children's heads by turn dropped backwards and fell upon their breasts, in ecstacy. The bells rang out; the choristers shouted their hymn of praise; the priest murmured:

"*Corpus Domini nostri Jesu Christ ...*"

The key tapped; and the angels kept leading new rows to the Holy Table and bringing the others away again.

And the great work went on in solemn silence amid all that jubilant music. The congregation were lifted up, their hearts throbbed and their tears welled with happiness and contentment.

The last row had come back; and they were all now kneeling in adoration when the head boy read out:

"What shall we return Thee, O Lord, for what Thou hast done for us! But now we were mute, prostrate in adoration, amazed and awed by Thy mighty presence in our hearts, bowed down in the dust of our humility; now at last we dare raise our heads and thank Thee. We beseech Thee that Thou wilt continue to dwell in our hearts, to reign there and to pour forth Thy mercies there abundantly. We are frail creatures; and, were it not that Thou, in Thy compassion, dost uphold us, we should continually and at every moment fall and succumb in the rude gusts of life. We put our trust in Thee and we know that Thou wilt succour us and that we shall enter the life everlasting. Amen."

It was over; and the congregation looked round impatiently to see how they could get out of church quickest. Their tears were dried and their thoughts were once more fixed on clothes, home, coffee and cakebread. After the last sign of the cross, the men crowded outside; the mothers sought their youngsters, kept them out of the crush for fear of accidents and marched triumphantly through the two rows of sightseers that stood on either side of the church-door. Now was the moment for showing-off, for congratulation and admiration on every side, till the children did not know which way to turn or what to say; and they were very hungry. All now went with their friends to the tavern for a drop of Hollands; and from there mother went home with two or three wives of the neighbourhood.

Horieneke walked behind. She was all by herself and wrapped in contemplation: that great miracle was now over, all of a sudden, and she could hardly believe it. Instead of enjoying all the happiness for which she had waited so long, her heart was full of distress and she felt inclined to cry. She had been so uneasy in church, so shy and frightened: there was the reading of that paper before all those people; and directly after, amid all the confusion, Our Lord had come. Hastily and very distractedly she had said her prayers, had spoken, asked and prayed and then waited for the miracle, waiting for Our Lord, Who now, living in her, would speak. And nothing had happened, nothing: she had done her very best to listen amidst the bustle outside and around her ... and yet nothing, nothing! Meanwhile she had raised her head to breathe ... and the people were leaving and she had to go with them: it was finished! It had all been so matter-of-fact, just like the communion-practice of yesterday, when she had merely swallowed a morsel of bread. Her heart beat in perplexity and she feared that she had made an unworthy communion.

The wind blew under her veil, which flew up in the air behind her. She was so pure, so unspotted in all that white; and, cudgel her brains as she would, she could not remember any fault or sin which she had omitted to confess. Though Our Lord had not spoken to her, He had been there all the same and she had not heard Him because of all that was happening around her. She ought to have been alone there, in a silent church. Even here, outside, by the trees, would have been better.

The wives were asked in to coffee and they stood and waited for Horieneke at the garden-gate. Indoors everything was anyhow: Fonske was going about in his shirt, Bertje had one leg in his breeches and Dolfke sat on the floor, playing with Trientje. Father had made coffee and stood with the bottles and glasses ready, looking dumbfounded at his child, now that he saw her for the first time in her white clothes. The boys crowded round shyly; they no longer knew their sister in this great lady; they kept hold of one another shyly, with their fingers in their mouths; they were unable to speak a word. Mother threw off her cloak and began cutting currant-bread and butter. Horieneke was made to take off her veil and gloves and a towel was fastened under her chin. The wives and youngsters sat down. First a drop to each; all drank to the health of the little first-communicant; they touched glasses. Father poured out and Horieneke had to drink too: she put the stuff to her lips, pulled a wry face and pushed the glass away. The boys dipped and soaked the bread in their coffee; and the wives started talking about their young days and about clothes and the old ways and the fine weather and the fruit-crop. Mother did nothing but cut fresh slices of bread-and-butter, which were snatched away and gobbled up on every side.

"Eat away!" said father.

The hostess of "The Four Winds" had been unable to take her eyes off Horieneke all through mass.

"Damned pretty, like a little angel!" said Stiene Sagaer.

"And a curly head of hair like a ball of gold! It made one's mouth water! And that wreath!" squealed the farmer's wife from the Rent Farm.

"Mam'selle Julie had a hand in it."

"And such pretty manners! Well, dear, Our Lord will be mighty pleased with you."

"And how nicely she read that piece!" said Stiene. "My blood crept when I heard it. Look here, Wanne Vandoorn was sitting beside me; and, you can take my word, the good soul couldn't control herself and we both cried till we sobbed."

"I felt it too," said mother. "Such things are cruel hearing. And the priest...."

"Ah, he knows how to talk, that holy man! He's a pure soul."

"You'll regret it all your days, Ivo, that you weren't there to see it."

Father nodded and took another slice of bread-and-butter.

"It'll take me all the week to tell about it at home," said the farmer's wife.

The boys sat making fun among themselves of Stiene Sagaer's crooked nose and the squeaky voice of the farmer's wife. When the wives had done eating, they stood up and went.

When they had gone some little way, they turned round again and cried against the wind:

"It's going to be fine to-day, Ivo!"

"And warm!" piped the farmer's wife. "Beautiful weather!"

They went down the sand-path, each wending her own way home.

The boys were now dressed and father, stripped to the waist, went out to wash his face under the trees at the pump. His freshly-ironed white shirt was brought out and his shiny boots and his blue smock-frock and black-silk cap. After much fuss and turning and seeking, he got ready and the boys too. Mother was busy with the baby in the cradle; Horieneke was showing her new holy pictures to Trientje; and Bertje and the other boys had gone out to play in the road. The bells rang again, this time for high mass. Many small things had still to be rummaged out, clothes to be pinned and buttoned; and the boys, with their Sunday penny in their pocket, marched up the wide road to high mass.

The wind had dropped and the sun blazed in the clear blue of the sky, which hung full of unravelled white cloud-threads, showing gold at the edges. A gay light lay over all the young green; the huge fields were full of waving corn, which swayed and bowed and straightened again, shining in streaks as under clear, transparent water. The trees stood turned to the sun, as though painted, so bright that from a distance one saw all the leaves, finely drawn, gleaming against the shadows that lay below. Here they stood in close hedges on either side of the road, trunk after trunk, making a dark wall with a dense roof of leafage, which presently opened out in a rift at the turn of the road, where four tree-trunks stood out against the sky; and then the trees turned away to the left and were drawn up in two new rows, which stretched out beside the road right across the plain. Here and there a few other trees stood lonely in the fields, gathered in small clumps, with the light playing between them; and far away at the edge of the bright expanse, in a wealth of mingled green, amid the tufted foliage with its changing hues and shadows, the little pointed church showed above the uneven, red-tiled roofs. It was all like a restful dream, made up of Sunday peace. Above and around, all the air was sounding with the gay tripping music of the three bells as they rang together: a laughing song in the glad sunshine, summoning from afar the people who came from every side, clad in their best. The boys, in their new red-brown, fustian breeches, standing stiff with the tailor's crease in them, and their thick, wide jackets and shiny hats, held father's hand or skipped round Horieneke, whom they could not admire enough. In the village square they hid themselves and went to the booth to see how they could best spend their pennies.

The people stayed in the street, looking about, and did not go into the church until the little bell tolled out its tinkling summons and the last little maid had been looked at and had disappeared. Then the men knocked out their pipes against the tips of their shoes and sauntered in through the wide church-door.

The incense still hung about the aisles and the sun sifted its golden dust through the stained-glass windows right across the church. The congregation stood crowded and crammed together behind their chairs, looking at the gilt of the flowers and at the great mountain of votive candles that were burning before the altar. The organ had all its pipes wide open; and music streamed forth in great gusts that resounded in the street outside. The priest sang and rough men's voices chanted the responses with the full power of their throats. And the high mass proceeded slowly with its pomp of movement and song. The congregation prayed from their books or, overcome by the heat, sat yawning or gazing at the incense-wreaths or started nodding on their chairs. The saints stood stock-still, smiling from their pedestals and proud in their high day finery. When the singing ceased, one heard through the dreamy murmur of the organ the spluttering of the burning candles and the clatter on the brass dish of the sacristan making the collection. The priest once more mounted the pulpit and, with the same gestures and action, delivered the same admonitions as earlier in the morning. Again the people sat listening and weeping; others slept. More organ-music and singing and praying and the mass came to an end and the priest turned to the congregation and gave the blessing. They streamed out of church in a thick crowd and stood in the road again to see the youngsters pass. Then all of them made their several ways to the taverns. The first-communicants had to call on aunts and cousins and friends; and the poorer children went to show their clothes and asked for pennies.

Horieneke and father and the brothers went straight home to await the visitors. Before they reached the door, they smelt the butter burning in the pan, the roast and the vegetables. The stove roared softly; and on the flat pipe stood earthen and iron pots and pans simmering and fretting and sending up clouds of steam to the rafters. Amidst it all, mother hurried to and fro in her heavy wooden shoes. Her body still waggled in her wide jacket and blue petticoat. Her face shone with grease and perspiration. She puffed and sighed in the intolerable heat. The blue chequered cloth lay spread on the table; and all around were the plates with the freshly tinned spoons and forks and little beer-glasses.[8] Outside, the boys sat in the top of the walnut-tree, waiting and peering for any one coming. Father had taken off his blue smock and turned up his shirt-sleeves and now went to see to his birds. That was his great hobby and his work on Sunday every week. All the walls were hung with cages: in that big one were two canaries, pairing; in the next, a hen-canary sitting on her eggs; and in a little wire castle lived a linnet and a cock-canary and three speckled youngsters. The finches were in a long row of darkened cages and moulting-boxes. When he put out his hands, the whole pack started singing and whistling; they sprang and fluttered against the bars and pecked at his fingers. He took the cages down one by one, put them on the table and whistled and talked to his birds, cleaned the trays and filled the troughs with fresh water and seed. The canary-bird got a lump of white sugar and the linnet half an egg, because of her young ones. Then he stood and watched them washing their beaks and wings and splashing in the water, pecking at their troughs now full of seed and at their sugar and cheerfully hopping on and off their perches. Then, when they were all hung up again in their places on the wall, they all started whistling together till the kitchen rang with it. The baby screamed in its cradle. Trientje cried and mother stamped across the floor in her heavy wooden shoes.

[8] The West-Flemings brew a beer so extremely strong that it is served in quite small glasses, not more than half the size of an ordinary tumbler.

"Hi, mates, I see something!" Fonske called from the walnut-tree.

The boys stretched their necks and so did father: it was jogging along in the distance, coming nearer and nearer.

"Uncle Petrus and Aunt Stanse in the dog-cart!"

They slithered out of the tree like cats and ran down the road as fast as they could. The others now plainly heard the wheels rattling and saw the great dogs tugging and leaping along as if possessed. High up in the car sat uncle, with his tall hat on his round head, bolt upright in his glossy black-broadcloth coat; and beside him broad-bodied Aunt Stanse, with coloured ribbons fluttering round her cap and a glitter of beads upon her breast. In between them sat Cousin Isidoor, half-hidden, waving his handkerchief. They came nearer still, jolting up and down through the streaks of shade and sunlight between the trees. Uncle Petrus flourished his hand, pushed his hat back and urged the dogs on; aunt sat with her face aflame and the drops of sweat on her chubby cheeks, laughing, with her hands on her hips, because of the shaking of her fat stomach. The dogs barked and leapt right and left at the boys. Petrus jumped nimbly out of the cart, ran along the shafts and led the team with a stylish turn out of the road, through the gate, into the little garden, where it pulled up in front of the door. The dogs stood still, panting and lolling out their tongues. Mother was there too and cried, "Welcome," and took Doorke under the armpits and lifted him out of the cart. Aunt began by handing out baskets, parcels and bundles. Then, sticking out her fat legs, in their white stockings, she climbed out of the cart and looked round at the youngsters, who already stood hankering to know what was in the basket.

"Well, bless me, Frazie, I needn't ask you how it goes with the chickens! There's a whole band of them and all sound and well: just look at them! Oh, you fatty!" And she pinched Bertje's red cheeks. "And you too, Frazie."

"Look at the state I'm in!" said mother, sticking her hands under the apron stretched tight across her fat stomach and looking down at her bare legs. "Such a heap to do, no time to dress yet."

"You're all right as you are, Frazie; you've no need to hide your legs nor t'other either: you've a handsome allowance of both," said Uncle Petrus, chaffingly. "I'd like a drop of water for the dogs, though."

Father sent the bucket toppling down the well and turned the handle till it rose filled. The dogs stuck their heads into the bucket and lapped and gulped greedily. Cousin stood staring bashfully amid all those peasant-lads and all that jollity, while Bertje, Fonske and the others too did not come near, but stood looking at the little gentleman with his fine clothes and his thin, peaky face; they trotted and turned, whispered to one another, went outside and came back again, laughed and said nothing.

"But the first-communicant! Where's Horieneke?" asked Stanse, suddenly.

From the little green arbour, in between the trees, a golden curly-head came peeping, followed by a little white body and little Trientje too, holding a great bunch of yellow daffodils in her hand. Stanse stuck out her arms in the air:

"Oh, you little butterfly! Come along here, you're as lovely as an angel!"

And she lifted Horieneke from among the flowers, right up to her beaded breast, and pressed her thick lips to the child's forehead with a resounding smack.

"Godmother, godmother," whimpered Trientje.

"Yes, you too, my duck!"

And the child forthwith received two fat kisses on its little cheeks.

The dogs were now unharnessed and father and Petrus had gone for a stroll in the orchard. The boys stood crowding against the table, looking at aunt undoing her parcels. In one were sweet biscuits, in another brandy-balls, peppermints, pear-drops and toffy. All this was carefully divided into little stacks and each child was given his share, with the strict injunction not to eat any before noon. Fonske hid his in the drawer, next to the canary-seed, Dolfke his in the cupboard and Bertje shoved his portion into his pockets. It was not long before three or four of them were fighting like thieves and robbers, while Stanse and Frazie went to look at the baby, which lay sleeping quietly in the cradle.

First one more drop of cherry-gin apiece and then to dinner. The soup stood ready ladled out, steaming in the plates. Horieneke sat demurely in the middle, next to Doorke, with uncle and aunt on either side and, lower down, father and all the children: mother had to keep moving to and fro, waiting on them, snatching a mouthful now and again betweenwhiles. When every one was served and Trientje had stammered out her

Our Father aloud, father once more stood up, as the master of the house, and said:

"You are all of you welcome and I wish you a good appetite."

The spoons began to clatter and the tongues to wag: uncle praised the delicious leek-soup, so did aunt; and then came endless questions from every side about the news of the district and all that had happened during the last ten or twelve years, ever since Frazie had married and left her home.

The children sat staring with wide-open eyes, now at their plates, now at aunt with her fat cheeks and her diamond cross that hung glittering at the end of a gold chain on her enormous breast; they counted the rings that were spitted on her fingers right up to the knuckles; they gazed at her earrings.... As the soup went down, the faces began to shine and mother pulled at her jacket and complained of the dreadful heat. Father pushed up the window and opened the back-door. The wind and the scented air, with pollen from the cherry-trees, now blew across the table and played refreshingly in their necks and ears. Mother kept on running about and serving: it was hot carrots now and boiled beef. Father took the flowered milk-jug and filled the little tumblers with beer. Slices of meat and fat were cut off with the big carving-knife and distributed; each received his plateful of glistening carrots; and the forks went bravely to work. After that, the great iron pot was set on the table, with the rabbits, which, roasted brown, lay outstretched in the appetizing, simmering gravy that smelt so good; and beside it a dish of steaming potatoes. The little tumblers were emptied and filled again; in between the loud talking you could hear the crunching of the teeth and the cracking of the bones; the children sat smeared to their eyes and picked the food in their plates with their hands. Uncle's eyes began to twinkle and he started making jokes, so much so that aunt had every moment to stop eating for laughing; then her broad head would fall backwards and her cheeks, which bloomed like ripe peaches, creased up and displayed two rows of gleaming ivory teeth. It all turned to a noisy giggling; and the general merriment could be heard far away in the other houses.

Uncle Petrus enjoyed teasing his sister and made her cry out each time he declared that, for all her waiting at table and running about, she had eaten more than he and Brother Ivo put together and that it was no wonder she had grown such a body and bred such fine youngsters. The mighty din woke the baby and started it crying loudly in its cradle. Fonske took it out and put it in mother's lap. It was as fresh and pink as a rose-bud; it kicked its little legs about and shoved its fists into its eyes.

"Yes, darling, you're hungry too, I expect."

And she unbuttoned her jacket and from behind her shift produced her great right breast. The baby stuck its hands into that wealth of whiteness, seized the proffered nipple in its mouth and started greedily sucking. After the first eager gulps it gradually quieted, closed its eyes and lay softly drinking, rocked on mother's heaving lap. Isidoorke kept looking at this as at something very strange that alarmed him. Horieneke, noticing it, held up a rabbit-leg to him and told him of those pretty white rabbits which she had seen slaughtered yesterday. The other youngsters had now eaten their fill and began to feel terribly bored at table. Bertje gave Fonske a kick on the shin and they went outside together, whispering like boys with some roguery in view. Wartje, Dolfke and the others followed them outside. When it was all well planned, they beckoned behind the door to Doorke; and, when the little man came out at last:

"Is it true, Doorke? Do you dare go among the dogs?"

And they led him on gently by his velvet jacket, behind the house to the bake-house, where the dogs lay blinking in the shade, with their heads stretched on their paws.

Doorke nodded; and, to show how well-behaved they were, he went close up to them and stroked their backs.

"And is it also true," asked Bertje, with mischievous innocence, "that you know how to harness them?"

Doorke looked surprised and again nodded yes.

"Let's see if you dare!"

"Hoo, hoo, Baron!" said Doorke.

And he took the dog by the collar, put the girths on him and fastened the traces while Fonske held up the cart.

"And that other one too?"

Doorke did the same with the other dog and with the third; and they were now all three harnessed. Bertje took the cart by the shafts and drew it very softly, without a sound, under the windows and through the little gate into the road. The other boys bit their fingers, held their breaths and followed on tip-toe. Then they all crept into the cart; and, when they were comfortably seated, Bertje took the reins and:

"Gee up!"

Wartje struck the dogs with the handle of the whip and they leapt forward lustily and the cart rolled along through the clouds of dust rising from the sandy road.

Horieneke had come up too and watched this silent sport; and she now stood alone with Doorke, looking along the trees, where the cart was disappearing towards the edge of the wood. When there was nothing more to see, they both went indoors.

Uncle and aunt and father were now talking quietly and earnestly, over three cups of coffee. Mother still sat with the baby on her lap, where it had fallen asleep while sucking. Aunt was constantly wiping the glistening perspiration from her forehead; and she unbuttoned her silk dress because she had eaten too much and her heart was beginning to swell.

"Shouldn't we be better out of doors?" she asked.

Mother tucked in her breast, buttoned her jacket and laid the child carefully in the cradle, near Trientje, who sat sleeping in her little baby-chair. They left everything as it was: table and plates and pots and glasses. Father and uncle filled their pipes and went outside under the elder-tree, in the shade. The wives tucked their clothes between their legs and lay down in the grass. Aunt had carefully rolled up her silk skirt and was in her white petticoat.

They now went on talking: an incessant tattle about getting children and bringing them up, about housekeeping and about land and sand and parish news, until, overcome by the heat and the weight of their bodies, they let their heads fall and closed their eyes and seemed to sleep. Uncle and father stood looking at them a little longer and then, in their white shirt-sleeves, with their thumbs in their tight trouser-bands, went up the narrow little path, in the blazing sun, to look at the wheat and the flax, which were already high.

Horieneke and Doorke were now left looking at each other. Horieneke began to tire of this; and she took the boy by the hand and led him into the house and up to her room. There she showed him her holy pictures on the wall and her little statues; they sat down side by side on the bed; and Horieneke told him the whole of her life and the doings of the last few days, all that she had longed for and to-day's happiness. The boy listened to her gladly; he looked at her with his big, brown eyes and sat still closer to her on the bed. He had now to see her pretty clothes; and they went together to the best bedroom where the veil lay and the wreath and her prayer-book and earrings. She must next really show him what she had looked like that morning in church; and he helped her put on the veil, placed the wreath on her curls and then took a few steps backwards to see. He thought her very pretty; and they smiled happily. Then everything was taken off again; and they went hand in hand, like a brother and sister who had not seen each other for some time, to walk in the little flower-garden. Here they looked at every leaf and named every flower that was about to open. When everything had been thoroughly inspected, they sat and chatted in the box arbour, very seriously, like grown-up people. Then they also became tired and Horieneke put her arm over Doorke's shoulder, allowed her golden curls to play in his eyes and in this way they walked out, down the road, towards the wood. Here they were all alone with the birds twittering in the trees and the crickets chirping in the grass beside the ditch.

Everywhere, as far as they could see, was corn and green fields and sunshine and stillness. They strolled down the long, cheerful road. Doorke held his arm round Horieneke's tight-laced little waist and listened to all the new things which his cousin described so prettily; and she too felt a great delight in having this boy, with his brown eyes and his lean shoulder-blades, beside her, listening to her and looking at her and understanding her ever so much better than her rough little brothers did. She would have liked to walk on all her life like this, in that golden sunshine, telling him how she had read that beautiful prayer in church this morning ... and about the priest's sermon ... and those pretty angels with their gold wings, who had walked up and down so calmly and placidly; about her dread during the communion-mass and her fear and sorrow because Our Lord had not spoken in her little heart. And so, talking and listening, they came to the wood. It looked so pleasant under those pollard alders in the shade and farther on in the dark, among the spruces, where the light filtered through in meagre rays, after that long walk in the blinding sun.

"Let's go in!" said Doorke and was on the point of going down the little path that ran beside the ditch, in among the trees.

"We mustn't!" said Horieneke; and she clutched him by the arm.

Her face grew very serious and she wrinkled her forehead:

"Look there!"

And she pointed through a gap between the trees down to the valley where, above the tall trunks, they could see the whole expanse of a big homestead, with the long thatched roofs of stable and barn and the tiles and slates of the house and turrets. She put her mouth to his ear and whispered:

"That's where the rent-farmer lives ... and he's a bad, bad man. He does wicked things to the little girls who go into the wood; and mother says that then they fall ill and die and then they go to Hell!"

Doorke did not understand very well, but he saw from Horieneke's wide-open eyes that it was serious. They sat down together on the edge of the ditch, with their legs in the grass, played with the daisies and listened to the thrushes gurgling deep down in the wood. They sat there for a long time. The sun sank to the top of the oak; the sky was flecked with white clouds which shot through the heavens in long diverging shafts, like a huge peacock's tail upon an orange field.

The children mused:

"I should like to fall down dead, here and now," said Horieneke.

Doorke looked up in surprise:

"Why, Horieneke?"

"Then I should be in Heaven at once."

They again sat thinking a little:

"Playing with the angels!... Have you ever seen angels, Doorke?"

"Yes, in the procession, Horieneke."

"Ah, but I mean live ones! I saw some last night, live ones; and they were in white, Doorke, with long trains and golden hair and diamond crowns, and they were singing in a beautiful garden!..."

With raised eyebrows and earnest gestures of her little forefinger, she told him all her dream of the angels and the swings and the singing and the music ... and of father with his sickle.

Doorke hung upon her words.

The thrush started anew and they sat listening.

"What will you do when you grow up, Doorke?"

And she put her arm round the boy's neck again and looked fondly into his eyes:

"Will you get married, Doorke?"

Doorke shook his head.

"Not even to me?"

And she looked at him with such a roguish smile that the boy felt ashamed. Then, to comfort him, she said:

"Nor I either, Doorke. Do you know what I'm going to do?"

"No, Horieneke."

"Listen, Doorke, I'll tell you all about it, but promise on your soul not to tell anybody: Bertje, Fonske and all the rest mustn't know."

Doorke nodded.

"Father wanted me to go into service down there, with all those wicked people. Then I cried for days and days and prayed to Our Lord; and mother told father that I was dying; and then she said that I might ... Try and guess, Doorke!"

Doorke made no attempt to guess. Then she drew him closer to her and whispered:

"Mother said I might stay at home and help her ... and afterwards, when I am grown up ... I shall become a nun, Doorke, in a convent; but first mother must get another baby, a new Horieneke.... And you?"

The boy didn't know.

"And you, Doorke, must learn to be a priest; then you and I will both go to Heaven."

Behind them, on the road, came a noise and a rush and an outcry so great that the children started up in fright. Look! It was Bertje and all the little brothers in the dog-cart, which was coming back home through the sand. When they saw cousin and Horieneke, they raised a mighty shout of joy and stopped. Bertje stood erect and issued his commands: all the boys must get out; he would remain sitting on the front seat, with Horieneke and Doorke side by side behind him, between two leafy branches, like a bride and bridegroom! Fonske cut two branches from an alder-tree and fastened them to either side of the cart. Then they set out, amid the shouting and cheering of the boys running in front and behind:

"Ready?"

"Ye-e-es!"

The dogs gave an angry jerk forward and the cart went terribly fast and Doorke clutched Horieneke with one hand and with the other warded off the hanging willow-twigs that lashed their faces.

The sun had gone down and a red light was glowing in the west, high up in the tender blue. The air had turned cooler and a cold, clammy damp was falling over the fields, which now lay steaming deadly still in the rising mist that already shrouded the trees in blue and darkened the distances.

At the turn of the road, the children stepped out of the cart and put it away carefully behind the bake-house, tied up the panting dogs and sauntered into the house.

"Father, we've been out with cousin," said Bertje.

They had to take their coffee and their cakebread-and-butter in a hurry: it was time to put the dogs in, said uncle.

Doorke said they were put in.

Frazie helped her sister on with her things:

"You'll find the looking-glass hanging in the window, Stanse. I must go and put on another skirt too and come a bit of the way with you."

The boys were to stay at home; they got the rest of the sweets and were ordered to bed at once. Horieneke was told to take off her best clothes; it was evening and the goats had still to be fed. She went to her little room reluctantly and could have cried because it was all over now and because it was so melancholy in the dark. She felt ashamed when she came down again and glanced askance at Doorke, who would think her so plain in her week-day clothes. The boy looked at her and said nothing; then he jumped into the cart and drove off slowly. Mother with Stanse and father with uncle came walking behind.

It was still light; the evening was falling slowly, slowly, as though the daylight would never end. In the west the sky was hung with white and gold tapestry against an orange background. On the other side, the moon, very wan still, floated in the pale-blue all around it. Beside the bluey trees long purple stripes of shadow now lay, with fallen clusters of branches, on the plain. You could hardly tell if day or night were at hand.

Uncle and aunt were extremely pleased with their visit; uncle looked contentedly into the distance and boasted that he had never seen such an evening nor such fine weather so early in the year, while Frazie at each step flung her arms into the air and stopped to say things to Stanse, whose good-natured laugh rang out over the plain and along the road. In front of them, Doorke, like a little black shadow, danced up and down in his cart to the jolting of the wheels as he jogged quietly along. The crickets chirped in the ditch; and from high up in the trees came the dying twitter of birds about to go to sleep.

Father wanted to drink a parting glass of beer in the Swan; Doorke could drive along slowly.

"Just five minutes then," said Petrus.

There were many people in the inn and much loud merriment. The new arrivals were soon sitting among the others, staying on and listening to all the jolly songs; and, when this had gone on for some time, they forgot the hour and the parting. Aunt Stanse held her stomach with laughing; she was not behindhand when the glasses had to be emptied or when her turn came to sing a song. Amid the turmoil, the rent-farmer came up to Frazie, took her impudently by the arm, laughingly wished her *proficiat* with her pretty daughter and, after slyly looking about him for confirmation, said, half in earnest:

"We're planting potatoes to-morrow at the Rent Farm, we shall want lots of hands; missie may as well come too."

And with that he went back to his game of cards.

This time, the leave-taking was genuine. Petrus got up; and it was good-bye till next year, when Doorke would make his first communion.

The cart was waiting outside the door; they stepped in, uncle took the reins.

"A safe ride home!"

"Thanks for the pleasant visit! And to our next merry meeting!"

"God speed!... Good-night!"

"Gee up!"

The dogs sprang forward, the cart rumbled along and soon the whole thing had become a shapeless black patch among the black trees. In the still night they could just hear the wheels rattling over the cobbles; and then Ivo and Frazie went home again.

A breeze came playing through the garden, sighing now and again with a sound as soft as silk; the moon shone upon the dark trees and its light played like golden snow-flakes dancing and fluttering down upon the gleaming crests of the green bushes and the milk-white plain. The air was heavy and stifling, full of warm damp; and strong-scented gusts of fresh, rain-laden perfumes blew across the road.

They stepped hurriedly on the legs of their long shadows and did not speak. There came a new rustling in the trees and a few big, cool drops of rain pattered on the sand, one here, one there and gradually quicker.

Ivo and Frazie hastened their pace; but, when the great drops began to fall on them thick as hail and around them in the sand, till the rain streaked through the air and rattled tremendously over their heads, mother held her body with both hands to prevent its shaking, Ivo tied his red handkerchief over his silk cap and they started running.

"It was main hot for the time of year."

"And the flowers smelt too strong and the thrush sang so loud."

It went on raining: a wholesome, cleansing downpour, a slow descent in slanting lines that glittered in the moonlight, bringing health to the earth. The air was fragrant with the wet grass and the white flowers: it was like a rich garden. At home, everything was put away, the table cleared and wiped; the lamp was alight and all the doors open. The boys were in bed. Horieneke had read evening prayers to them and then hurried to her little room, to be alone; and there she had lain thinking of all that had happened during that long day: her jaws ached from the constant smiling; and she felt dead-tired and sad.

Father took off his wet blouse and mother stirred up the fire: they would have one more cup of coffee, with a drop of something, and then go to bed. Ivo lit his pipe and stretched out his legs to dry beside the stove.

They drank their coffee and listened to the steady breathing of the boys and the dripping of the gutters on the cobbles outside. Father made a remark or two about uncle and aunt and about their village, but got only half-answers from his wife. Then, all of a sudden, he asked:

"What did the farmer come and say to you?"

Frazie sighed:

"They're planting potatoes to-morrow and we were to go and work; and Horieneke was to come too."

"Ay."

"But she'll stay here!"

"What do you mean, stay here?"

"Yes, she's got her work to do at home."

"All right; but if she has to go?"

"Don't care."

And mother stood with her arms akimbo, looking at her husband, waiting for his answer.

"And if he turns us out and leaves us without work!"

"And suppose our child comes home with a present ... from that beast of a farmer!"

Ivo knocked out his pipe:

"Pooh, that could happen to her anywhere; and, after all, she won't be tied to her mother's apron-strings all her life long!... When you live in a man's house and eat his bread, you've got to work for it and do his will: the master is the master. Come, let's go to bed; we've a lot to do tomorrow."

Suppressed sobs came from the little bedroom. Mother looked in. Horieneke lay with her hands before her eyes, crying convulsively.

"Well, what's the matter?"

The child pressed her head to the wall and wept harder than ever.

"Come along, wife, damn it! It's time that all this foolery was over, or she'll lose her senses altogether."

Mother grew impatient, bit her teeth:

"Oh, you blessed cry-baby!"

And angrily she thumped the child on the hip with her clenched fist and left her lying there.

"A nice thing, getting children: one'd rather bring up puppies any day!"

She turned out the light and it was now dark and still; outside, the thin rain dripped and the white blossoms blew from the trees and the whole air smelt wonderfully good. In the distance, the nightingale hidden in the wood jugged and gurgled without stopping; and it was like the pealing of a church-organ all night long.

* * * * *

The weather had broken up and the day dawned with a melancholy drizzle and a cold wind. The sky remained grey, discharging misty raindrops which soaked into everything and hung trembling like strung pearls on the leaves of the beech-hedge and on the grass and on the cornstalks in the fields. It was suddenly winter again. On the hilly field the people stood black, wrapped up, with their caps drawn over their ears and their red handkerchiefs round their necks. The hoes went up in the air one after the other and struck the moist earth, which opened into straight furrows from one end to the other of the field. Here wives walked barefoot, bent, with baskets on their arm from which they kept taking potatoes and laying them, at a foot's distance, in the open trench. In a corner of the field stood the farmer, his big body leaning on a stick; and his dark eyes watched his labourers.

There, in the midst of them, was Horieneke, bent also like the others, in her coarse workaday clothes, with a basket of seed-potatoes on her arm; and her red-gold curls now hung, like long corkscrews, wet against her face; and every now and then she would draw herself up, tossing her head back to keep them out of her eyes.

VI

IN THE SQUALL

At noon, under the blazing sun, all three started for the wood, after blackberries.

Trientje was in her cotton pinafore, with a straw hat on her head and a wicker basket on her arm. Lowietje stood in his worn breeches and his torn shirt; in his pocket he had a new climbing-cord. Each dragged Poentje by one hand, Poentje who still went about in his little shirt and, with his wide-straddling little bare legs, trotted on between brother and sister.

They went along narrow, winding foot-paths, between the cornfields, high as a man, through the flax-meadows and the yellow blinking mustard-flower. The sun bit into Lowietje's bare head and sent the sweat trickling down his cheeks.

They went always on, with their eyes fixed upon that thick crowd of blue trees full of blithe green and of dark depths behind the farthermost trunks.

Poentje became tired and let himself be dragged along by his hands. When he began to cry, they sat down in the ditch beside the corn to rest. Trientje opened her basket and they ate up all their bread-and-butter. Near them, in the grass, ants crept in and out of a little hole. Lowietje poked with a stick and the whole nest came crawling out. The children sat looking to see all those beasties swarm about and run away with their eggs.

All three stood up and went past the old mill, then through the meadow and so, at last, they came to the wood and into the cool shade. On the banks of the deep, hollowed path, it all stood thick as hail and black with the brambleberries. Lowietje picked, never stopped picking, and put them one by one in his mouth; and his nose and cheeks were smeared with red, like blood. Trientje steadily picked her whole basket full and Poentje sat playing on the way-side grass with a bunch of cornflowers.

In the wood, everything was still: the trees stood firmly in the blaze of the sun and the young leaves hung gleaming, without stirring. A bird sat very deep down whistling and its song rang out as in a great church. Turtle-doves cooed far away. Round the children's ears hummed big fat bees, buzzing from flower to flower. When the bank was stripped, they went deeper into the wood, Lowietje going ahead to show the way. They crept through the trees where it twilighted and where the sun played so prettily with little golden arrows in the leafage; from there they came into the high pine-wood. Look, look! There were other boys ... and they knew where birds lived!

"Listen, Trientje," said Lowietje. "You stay here with Poentje: I'll come back at once and bring your pinafore full of birds' eggs ... and young ones."

He fetched out his climbing-cord and, in a flash, all the boys were gone, behind the trees. Trientje heard them shout and yell and, a little later, she saw her little brother sitting high up on the slippery trunk of a beech. She put her hands to her mouth and screamed:

"Lo - wie!..."

It echoed three or four times over the low shoots and against the tall trees, but Lowietje did not hear.

A man now came striding down the path; he carried a gun on his shoulder. The boys had only just seen him and, on every side, they came scrambling out of the tree-tops, slid down the trunks and darted into the underwood. Breathless, bewildered and scared to death, Lowietje came to his sister and, with his two hands, held the rents of his trousers together:

"There were eight eggs there, Trientje, but the keeper came and, in the sliding, my trousers...."

And he let a strip fall. They were torn from end to end, from top to bottom, in each leg.

"Mother will be angry," said Trientje, very earnestly.

She took some pins from her frock and fastened the tears, so that the skin did not show.

Suddenly fell a rumbling thunder-clap that droned through all the wood and died away in a long chain of rough sounds. The children looked at one another and then at the trees and the sky. All stood black now, the sun was gone and a warm wind came working through the boughs, by gusts. It grew dark as night and at times most terribly silent.

And now - they all crossed themselves - a ball of fire flew through the sky and it cracked and broke and it tore all that was in the wood. The wind came up, the branches rocked and writhed and the leaves fluttered and tugged and heavy drops beat into the sand.

"Quick, quick!" said Trientje. "It's going to lighten!"

Lowietje said nothing and Poentje cried. Each took the child by one hand and they ran as fast as they could to get from under the trees.

"Ooh! Ooh!"

They dashed their hands before their eyes and stood still: a golden snake twisted round a tree and all the wood was bright with fire and there came a droning and a rumbling and a banging as of stones together and a hundred thousand branches burst asunder. Shivering, not daring to look up, they crossed themselves again and all three crept under the branches, deep down in a ditch. Trientje tied her pinafore over the little one's face and they sat there huddled together, shuddering and peeping through their fingers and saying loud Our Fathers.

"You must not look, Lowietje: the lightning would strike you blind."

The trees wrung their heavy boughs and everything squeaked and rustled terribly. The water rained and poured from the leafy vault on Trientje's straw hat, on Lowietje's bare head and right through his little torn shirt. And clap and clap of thunder fell; the sky opened and belched fire like a hot oven. The children sat nestling into each other's arms - Poentje down under the other two - and only when it had kept still for long did they all, trembling and terrified, dare to put out their heads.

"I wish we were home now!" sighed Lowietje.

Once more the sky was all on fire and rumbling and breaking and crackling till the earth quaked and shook.

"O God, O God, help us get out of the wood and home to mother!" whined Trientje.

When they opened their eyes again, they saw below them, in the bottom, a huge beech with a bough struck off and the white splinters bare, with leaves awkwardly twisted right round: it stood there like a fellow with one arm off.

The rain now fell steadily in straight stripes; the noise grew fainter and the sky broke open.

Soaked through with the wet, the children came creeping out of the ditch and now, holding their breaths, stood looking at that tree which was so awesomely cleft and at that crippled bough which hung swinging over space. The thunder still rumbled, but it was very far away, like heavy waggons rattling over hard stones. Lowietje caught his little brother up on his back and they made straight for the opening of the drove, where they saw a clear sky. They must get out of the wood, away from those trees where such fearful things happened and where it cracked so and where it was so dark.

Outside, the heaven hung full of gold-edged clouds and the sun drove its bright darts through the sky. The rain fell in lovely gleaming drops and all looked so new, so fresh and so strangely glad as after a fit of weeping, when the glistening tears hang in laughing eyes. 'Twas all so peaceful here and 'twas far behind them that the trees were twisted and bent. Here and there flew birds; and the cuckoo sat calling in a cornfield. Lowietje's shirt was glued to his skin; his trousers hung heavily from his limbs and his hair fell in dripping tresses, sticking along his cheeks. The white spots on Trientje's pinafore were run through with the black; and wet cornstalks whipped her little thin skirt. Poentje splashed with his naked little feet in the puddles and asked for mother.

"We're almost home, child," said Trientje, to soothe him.

They went through the wet grass and fragrant cornfields along the slippery footpaths to a big road.

Look, there, behind the turning, came mother: she had a sack-cloth over her head and two umbrellas under her arm; she looked angry and ugly.

"We shall get a beating," sighed Lowietje.

VII

A PIPE OR NO PIPE

He dropped his wheel-barrow, strode from between the shafts and went and looked into the great window of the tobacco-shop. His eyes were all full, as far as they could carry: an abundance and a splendour to dream about. He came a step nearer and rested his two elbows on the stone window-sill, to see more comfortably.

Two stacks of motley cigar-boxes stood on either side and ran together at the top into a rounded arch, from which hung long, long pipes, cinnamon-wood pipes, as thick as your arm, with green strings to them and huge, big bowls, artfully carved into the heads of the King, of hideous niggers, or of pretty girls with beads for eyes.

On thick, transparent glass slips lay whole files of meerschaum pipes, furnished with clear curved-amber mouthpieces: fishes' heads, lobster-claws holding an eggshell, horses' heads, cows' hoofs; rich cigar-holders of meerschaum, all over silver stars and gold bands. Heaps and heaps and lots and lots of every kind, as far as he could see; and all this was multiplied in two enormous mirrors, in which, yonder, far back among all this smoking-gear, he saw his own face staring at him out of his great, astonished eyes.

He sighed. It was all so beautiful, so rich! And now if mother had only got work!

He went over it once more. Down below, in little plush-lined trays, lay the small pipes, the boys' stuff. They lay scattered higgledy-piggledy, whole handfuls of them, crooked and straight, brown and black. His eyes thieved round voluptuously in those trays and they read with eager curiosity the neatly-written figures which informed the world how much each pipe cost.

Here, they were crooked, comical little things of black cocus-wood; there, they were motley, speckled round bowls, like birds' eggs, with white stems; but they cost too much. And yet they were so charitably beautiful! Now his eyes remained hankering after a splendid varnished bowl. It was almost tucked out of sight, but it glittered so temptingly and had a lovely brown ring at the edge, shading downwards to a pale gold-yellow: there was a little cup for the oil to sweat into and a fat cinnamon stem, with a horn mouthpiece. He examined it on every side and would have liked to turn it over with his eyes. Inside the bowl stood, in black figures:

"1 *fr*. 50."

"Mother!..."

That was the one he wanted, that was his. She had promised him a pipe if she got work to-day. If only she had brought work with her!

After one last look and one more ... he went on.

He caught up his barrow and pushed it, over the wide

road, straight to the station.

There he had to wait.

He loitered round the dreary, deserted yard. The noon sun bit the naked stones; and everything, hiding and shrinking from that glowing sun-fire, seemed dead. The drivers sat slumbering on the boxes of their cabs; the horses stood on three legs, their heads down, crookedwise between the shafts, and now and then they gave a short stamp, to keep off the flies, which were terribly active. A group of loafers lay sleeping on their stomachs in the shade. A slow-moving vehicle drove past and disappeared round the corner. A dog came stepping up lazily and went and lay under the sunflowers near the signal-box, blinking his eyes.

There was nothing more that moved.

At last the train came gliding in very gently, without noise, and it sent a gulp or two of white smoke into the quivering blue sky.

Now the boy stood stretching his neck through the railings, on the look-out for his mother, whom he already saw in his thoughts, coming bent, with a heavily-laden bag of weaving-stuff; and the pipe was in his pocket ... or else nothing, nothing at all!

'Twas a fat gentleman that got out first; then a tall, thin one; then a woman; then another woman; always others; and now, now it was mother. She stuck out her thin leg, groping from the high foot-board to find the ground, and ... she had an empty blue-and-white canvas bag on her shoulder. His lower lip dropped sadly and he turned slowly to his barrow:

"No work yet. God better it!"

The mother threw her bag on the wheel-barrow and they went on, without speaking.

Straight opposite the tobacco-shop, the boy gave a sidelong glance at the great window, with all those rich things displayed behind it, and he whistled a little tune.

They had still far, very far to go, before they two were at home, in their village. And the sun was burning.

VIII

ON SUNDAYS

In his Sunday best! A red-and-yellow flowered scarf was tied round his sun-burnt neck and the two ends blew over his shoulders; a small brown-felt hat with a curly brim was drawn down upon his head and, from under it, came here and there a wisp of flaxen hair. He wore a small, open jacket, with a short waistcoat, from under which a clean blue shirt bulged out; and his long, much too long trousers fell in wide folds over his big cossack shoes.[9] Under his arm he carried a bundle knotted into a red handkerchief, while with the other hand he twirled a switch.

[9] Hob-nailed shoes fastened with straps.

He was a growing youngster, a well-set-up cowherd, with a brown, freckled face, small, pale-grey eyes, under milk-white eyebrows, and bony knees and elbows: a sturdy fellow in the making.

'Twas heavenly, grand Sunday weather: it shone with light and life and it was all green, pale, splendid green, against a clear blue sky in the middle of the afternoon.

He stepped on bravely, along the wide drove of elms, twisting his switch, and looked into the free sky with his young, grey-blue eyes. He thought ... of what? Of nothing! Truly, of nothing: what does a cowherd think of? Wait a bit, though; he was thinking: 'twas Sunday! It was Sunday once more, the glad Sunday! And there were so few Sundays in those long, long weeks. And he was going home for a few hours: yes, home; and from there to Stafke's and to Stafke's pigeons.

He was hard-worked at the farm: twenty-nine cow-beasts, which were always hungry and always wanted fattening; furthermore, a whole herd of calves and hogs: 'twas a drudging without end or bottom, from early morning to late at night, until his limbs hung lame.

The farmer was good but strict and could not abide sluggards; he looked for work, hard work; and this the lad was glad to give, but only while looking forward to the everlasting Sunday, in which lay all his happiness and cheer.

He quickened his steps; and the elms pushed by, one by one, and at last, ahead, very far down that dark hedge of stems and leafage, came a tiny opening where the trees seemed to touch one another.

Look! There, beside the little village church, stood Farmer Willems' homestead, with its little slate turret and the great poplars and, beside it, close together and quite hidden in the green, two little cottages. 'Twas there that he was brought up and had grown up; there, in one of those cottages. In the other lived Stafke's father and mother. The children had led the half-wild life of the country there: two little boys together. They had clambered up those mighty trees, weltered in the sand of the drove and coursed like foals in the meadow. The farm was a free domain to them; they were at home in it; they went daily to the little door of the wash-house to fetch their slice of rye-bread-and-butter and, in the morning, an apple or a pear. They had lain and rolled in the hay-loft, like fish in the water; but all that had passed so quickly, so very quickly. The parish-priest came; and, for six months, six long months, they had had to go to school and church. Then, on a certain Monday morning, father said:

"Lad, you're coming along to the farm to-day, to bind corn."

Play was over, the free play of the country! They were pressed into labour, were saddled with the labourer's heavy burden. Since then, it had been an endless roving after work, from one farm to another, with his bundle under his arm.

Stafke had remained serving at Willems', with father, and he, on Sunday afternoons, had not so far to go, under the burning sun, in order to get home.

The way was long for an unthinking lad; and they seemed endless, those never-changing rows of tree-trunks, those uncounted yellow, blinking cornfields ... and never a creature on the road. It was something very much out of the way when a pigeon flew through the azure sky; the lad stood still and, turning round, followed the great ring which it made until it dropped far away, yonder among the houses of the village. Then he went on, pondering, as he went, that there was nothing, absolutely nothing lovelier than a milk-white pigeon in a pale-blue sky; and he whispered:

"Perhaps it's Stafke's pigeon."

On reaching home, he laid down his bundle; his baby sister came running up to him, with her little arms wide open, and held him by his legs; and he lifted her twice, three times above his head. He handed mother his earnings; and then, out of the door, to Stafke's!

"Roz'lie, is he in?"

"Oh, yes, he's up in the loft, with the pigeons."

He climbed up the ladder, in three steps and as carefully as he could, to the dovecote. Behind a swarm of half-stretched and loose-hanging clouts and canvas things, a lad sat on an overturned tub, his fair-haired curly head in his hands, his elbows on his knees, peering through a sort of lattice-work. Jaak sat down at the other side, on a bundle of maize, in just the same attitude, and looked too....

There were white, snow-white, mottled, blue, slate-blue, russet, speckled, grey, black-flecked, striped and spotted pigeons, doves, pouters - some cocks, the rest hens - a motley crowd all mixed up together. There were some that sat murmuring one to the other, softly - oh, so softly - and nodding their heads for sheer kindliness. Others cooed loudly, angrily or indifferently and tripped round one another. Others sat huddled, meditating, lonely and forlorn, blinking their bright little glittering eyes.

Through the holes, from the resting-board, new ones came walking in with shy feet and sought a little place for themselves; others passed out through the narrow opening and, flapping their wings, rose into the sky.

'Twas a humming and muttering without end, a murmuring and whispering loud and soft and a restless stir and movement: a little world full of neatly-dressed damsels, who were all so lightly, so prettily decked out and who knew how to manage their trains and their fine clothes so demurely and so comically. They carefully combed and cleaned their black velvet ruffs, smoothed their sharp-striped feathers one by one, fondled and rubbed their downy breasts till they shone like new-blown roses....

And Jaak and Stafke sat watching this, sat watching this, like two steel statues, sweating in that warm loft. They did not stir nor speak a single word.

And that lasted and went on....

It grew dusk. From every side the pigeons came flying in, whole troops of them, and sought their well-known roosts. They stood two and two, closely crowded together on the perches or huddled in the holes. They drew their heads into their feathered throats and slept. The rumour diminished to just a soft mumbling; and then nothing more. The pigeon that sat over there, squatting low on her eggs, faded from sight in her dark corner; and the whole upper row vanished in the dusk of the rafters.

The boys still sat on.

The dovecote became a pale-grey twilight thing, with drab and black patches here and there. The soft humming passed into a faint buzz that died away quite; and all was silence.

They both together stood up straight, gave a

long-drawn sigh and went below.

"It's getting dark," said Jaak, wiping the sweat from his face. "The cows will be waiting."

"Yes," said Stafke. "It gets evening all at once. Well, Jaak, till Sunday."

And Jaak went away, through the now moonlit drove, with a new bundle under his arm and thinking of the farm, of his twenty-nine cow-beasts and of Sunday and of Stafke's pigeons....

* * * * *

Il y a des malheurs qui arrivent d'un pas si lent et si sur qu'ils paraissent faire partie de la vie journaliere.

MONTALEMBERT.

IX

AN ACCIDENT

He had been half awake several times already, but each time he had slipped back into an uneasy doze, a restless, wearisome sojourn in a strange, drowsy world, in which he struggled with stupid, silly dream-spectres, all jumbled together in a huddled mass of incoherent, impossible thoughts and actions; a blank world in which all his workaday doings were forgotten; an after-life of tiring sleep following on the carouse of yesterday. He lay half-suffocated in the stifling heat of that tiled garret, lay tossing on a straw mattress. And suddenly, with a jolt that jerked him sleeping like a beast of burden. And now why couldn't he take life as it came, like his mates, who just went through it anyhow, without any calculating, callously and cheerfully, something like a machine which, when the sun comes out and it is daylight, begins to move arms and legs, to twist and turn the whole day long and, when it is evening again and dark, falls down and remains lying dead, for a few hours, with all the other things?

He drew himself up, thrust his thin legs into his trousers, his arms into a dirty jacket and let his weary limbs carry him below. His mother had buttoned up the linen satchel with his two slices of bread-and-butter and had ladled out his porridge. He went out followed by a "God guard you, lad!" and the little woman looked after her boy till he had vanished out of the alley. She was so fond of him, he knew it; yes, he knew all about that tender love, which he so often rejected in a moment of churlish impatience; but still he was sorry afterwards, even though he never showed it. That prim, old-fashioned little woman, with her cramped ways, was his mother; his father had been a drunkard and had been killed at his work: that was his parentage; it was their fault that he led this poverty-stricken existence.

He walked on, without looking up at all the swarming life around him, went step by step over the slippery cobbles, straight to his work. His work: why must he work, always that everlasting toiling, while others lived and enjoyed their lives without doing anything? He too had once thought - but it was only a dream - of becoming something; he had felt something stirring just there, inside him, and that seed would have sprouted and blossomed if they had only tended it; but they had ruthlessly repelled him, had refused to take him up with them on the heights; and he had remained in the mud, alone, all alone.

There it rose before him: a mighty edifice in building, with behind it a radiant summer sun that blazed forth high above the framework of the roof in the morning sky and made that giant structure stand black in its own shadow.

That was his work. All that mass of bricks he had seen grow into the mighty whole; and there it stood now, a huge block, with heavy, massive outlines, contained - held upright, it seemed - by a jumble of dirty-white stakes and posts, crossed and criss-crossed with planks. Out of a dirty hodge-podge of crazy houses, walls black with smoke, little inner rooms which for the first time saw the white light of day, with ragged strips of wall-paper and whitewash among rotten beams and rafters straight and askew, all of which his stubborn labour had made to fall and disappear, and out of those deep-dug foundations, out of that drudging in the dirty ground, those stout walls had grown stone by stone, had risen high into the sky - oh, the hard work of it! - and, tapering by degrees, had shot up to form that mighty building. Wall by wall, wrought at and toiled at, held together by pillars running beside narrow pointed windows to those peaked gable-steps, running into a forest of masts, of slanting beams that had to bear the roof, the whole of that sprawling monster had gradually acquired a sense and a meaning and become the splendid masterpiece that now stood there, solidly fixed against the blue sky like a magic crystallized phrase.

That beginning all over again, day after day, at the same work; all that busy stir of men and stones, now high in the air, now deep below; that incessant climbing up and down those swaying ladders: all this had made such a deep impression on him, had implanted itself into him so firmly that at the first sight of it he felt smitten with impotence, with a mechanical discouragement that gripped his whole being and made him work throughout the day as though urged by an all-ruling deity set there in the symbolic shape of that giant colossus at which he toiled. It seemed to him that he was an indispensable little part of that great building, a small moving thing with but a tiny atom of intelligence - sometimes - and fatally dragged along in that whirling circle, under the behest of the masters, who knew their way through every stroke and line of the great plan, who had all that great work in their heads and on paper and who possessed the power to bring all that complicated machine into operation. And he just went to work like a dog, set going by the mournful knocking of the stone-chopper, the shrill screech of the toothless iron marble-saw and all the banging and knocking and hewing up yonder at the top of things. He took his wooden hod, filled it with bricks and slowly climbed the ladder. He was once more the dismal noodle of last week, the hypnotized bag-o'-nerves that let himself be swept along in the whirlwind of habit and vexation, dazed by that awful hugeness which he was helping to complete and driven on by the ever-pursuing pair of eyes of his strict foreman. And his head ached so; and he felt so sick; and his legs bent under the load.

On he had to go and on. His head no longer took part in the work; his legs kept on going up and down the rungs with those bricks, those everlasting bricks: he did not know how many, just hauled them up, without stopping.

It seemed to him sometimes that the whole mass of walls and scaffolding, labourers and foremen made but a single being: a sort of fearsome deity, something like an unwieldy monster with inhuman, cruel feelings, something which had to be fed with all that workmen's sweat; and all this feverish activity seemed to him the whirling along of a crowd of unfortunates who had stepped into the fatal circle marked out for them, never to leave it again. Everything seemed so unsteady to-day: those walls on which he had to walk tottered; and he took such a pleasure in looking, in looking for a long time down below, yonder where the men and women were like ants and the great blocks of freestone became little bricks. It gave him such a delicious wriggling in the bowels, a tickling in his blood; and he felt his hair tingling on his head. Was not this the way to obtain release from that hard labour, to get out of that brain-racking circle?

Then he held on to a post until he recovered his senses; and he went down again for more bricks. It came from all that beer.

Yesterday had been a holiday. The wooden framework of the roof was finished; and they had nailed the May-bough to the top, the joyous emblem of difficulties vanquished. It showed up grandly there, with its bright green leaves so high in the air. The masters had granted the men a day off and given them plenty of beer. All that warm day they had made merry, drinking and singing and loafing about the streets like happy savages. He too had revelled with the rest, had been overcome by the drink and joined in everything, from the horseplay in the open air to the bestial amusements in those dark holes where the populace seeks its pleasure, that stimulant for the work of the morrow. Then that brutal drunkenness had come, with the loss of all his senses, till he found himself, dog-tired, sick and feverish, up in his garret under the tiles.

To-day the work was twice as irksome. That rising warmth which, in the morning, while it is still cool, forebodes the stifling, paralysing heat of the scorching noon-day, tortured his throat and his bowels; he couldn't go on.

"Slacker!" was the first word flung at his head. He stood on the high gable-steps and set down his load of bricks. That "Slacker!" played about in his head like the smarting pain of a lash. He stood looking aimlessly into space, indifferent to all that moved and lived around him. A shudder ran through his body. The wall tottered ... and he was so high up, all alone, seen by nobody: such a small creature in that blue sky, in that endless space. In a clear vision he saw his own figure in all its lean wretchedness, cut out like a paper silhouette, standing out sharply against the sky, such a miserable little object: two thin legs, like laths, a little stomach, two little sticks of arms and that small, everyday, vulgar head. Was that he, that tiny atom of this mighty, colossal building, that ant on the back of this behemoth ... which had only to move to shake him off, ever so low down!

Ah, here's that delicious wriggling in the bowels again! He has looked down. Once more. That's capital: something like a feeling of wanting to jump down, such an airy, irresponsible joy, like flying in a dense, blue sky, falling very gently and slowly - oh, what fun! - and then being rid of all one's troubles!... And yet there was a certain fear about it. He mustn't look any more. Or just this once ... that was grand! Once more that awful depth, with all those tiny figures, yawned below him; and it was the little wall that kept him up there so high, only that little wall.... One movement, the least little yielding, the least bending over: oh, what bliss ... and how frightful!... He became drunk with delight, filled with the pleasure of it; he gasped, his eyes became unseeing; it was like being wafted along, a gentle flight through the air and ... he fell.

Bumping against a scaffold, clutching with hands and feet; a breaking plank, a ghastly yell ... and then a body with arms and legs outspread in space, a thunderbolt ...

a thud as of a bag of earth ... and there he lay, stretched at full length, like a man asleep. That scream of distress, that terrible shriek, that farewell cry of one who is going away for good had sent something like an electric shock through all around; work ceased and they scrambled down and stood in a great circle around that body ... looking. And a great silence followed, that silence which is so heavy and oppressive after the sudden stop of so much activity. People came rushing up, pushing to get closer ... and to see. They tore the poor devil's clothes open to find out where he was hurt, others ran for help, while fresh swarms of folk came crowding up and the silence died in an uproar of questions and tramping and the wailing of women. He lay there, with his peaceful face turned to one side, lay on his back, seemingly uninjured; a few drops of blood trickled from his mouth. His eyes were closed like those of a man asleep.

"Such a height to fall!... So young, only a boy!"

Others stood chattering loudly, indifferently, as though about an everyday occurrence, or looked up at the wall and showed one another from where he had tumbled down.

There was a sudden movement in the crowd; people jostled one another.

"His mother's coming!" somebody whispered.

They pressed closer and closer to watch the effect upon her, the women with an anguished consciousness of what she must be suffering, that mother-pain which they understood so well. The men pushed to see what happened, because everybody was looking. All eyes were fixed on the little woman who came running along, with those elderly little hurried steps, those two anxious eyes which showed all the dread of the tragedy they suspected. The people made way respectfully, as before one who is privileged to approach and look upon what is hers. Those who could not move back she dragged away mercilessly, gripping them with her hooked fingers, which she thrust out at every side in order to see closer. It was her ... her ... her son lying there, her own son; and she must get to him.

She saw him. He lay there and he was dead, the son, the child whom she had seen leaving that morning alive and well. She stood aghast, out of breath after the great effort of hurrying, her throat pinched with distress and sorrow and shock, her soul filled with all the pent-up tempest that was seeking an outlet. Her flat chest heaved and all her thin, frail little body quivered; her legs shook beneath her. Slowly and painfully the sobs came welling up.

The people waited in silence, more or less disappointed, saddened by all that silent grief. Her eyes, the eyes of a mother, stared at the dead body; and he did not look at her and he slept on and ... and he was asleep for ever, gone for ever: he would never see her again! This last cut into her soul; a shrill scream came from her throat, she flung her lean brown hands together high above her head, wrung the crooked, gnarled fingers convulsively and then, with her fists clenched in her lap, sank impotently to her knees, with her head against his.

"Oh, it's such a pity, oh, it's such a pity!" she moaned; and the words contained all the awful depth of her woe, all the concentrated sorrow. "Oh, it's such a pity, such a pity!" she kept on repeating, finding no other words to express her grief and lending them power by force of repetition.

He remained lying there ... and she remained kneeling; and all that crowd of people stood silently looking on, startled and impressed by that sacred, solemn mourning. And the impressive hush, the silence of all those people, the desperate helplessness of those folk, she alone suffering and crying and unable to help her child and the people unwilling to help him: that impotence pierced her soul; and the patient suffering changed into a frenzied madness, a raging fury. With a terrible scream, like that of a goaded beast, a hoarse yell that came grating out of her parched throat, she thrust her arms, stiff with pain, like two steel rods, under the arms of that limp corpse and, with a superhuman effort, with Herculean strength exalted by suffering, she lifted the corpse, pressed it to her body, raised it with her outstretched arms and dragged it, with its legs trailing behind it, hurrying along at a mad pace, with the one idea of getting home with her child, her only child, away, far away from that callous crowd which desecrated her sorrow: there she would weep, sob out all her grief and find words, sweet words which must throb through her child and wake him and bring him back to life!

All that packed crowd had first followed her with their eyes, struck by the sudden outburst of that mad rage; and then they had gone after her, inquisitively. And it did not last long before the police-constables - those phlegmatic posts with which any outbreak of undue human emotion must always in the end collide - stopped them; they pulled those bony arms from round the corpse and took the little mother, now hanging slack and limp, one on either side by the arm and led her away. The body was carried to the mortuary.

With a resounding oath the foreman drove his folk back to work and set all that rolling activity going once more.

The passers-by hastened away; and the saw screeched, the chisel tapped, the hammer banged, the bricks were hauled up on high and the gorgeous building, the pride of a metropolis, stood resplendent in the glaring white mid-day sun, as if nothing had happened.

X

WHITE LIFE

Her life flowed on as a little brook flows under grass on a Sunday noon in summer, flowed on in calm seclusion, far from the bustle of the crowd, secretly, steadily, uninterrupted save by ever-recurring little incidents, peacefully approaching old age. She sat in her little white room, behind the muslin curtains, making lace. Her cottage stood a little way back from the street, shining behind a neatly-raked flower-garden.

The door was always shut and the curtains carefully drawn. Inside, everything was very clean: smooth, bare walls and the ceiling washed with milk-white chalk through which shone a soft touch of blue; and this bright cleanliness contrasted soberly with the things that hung on the wall. The chairs and furniture stood placed with care, as though nailed to the floor; over the mantel hung the copper Christ, a thin, elongated figure of Our Lord, with its sharp projections which shone when the sun touched them: a little figure which, so long dead, hung there so firmly nailed and looked so calmly from out of the small dark shadow-lines of its face.

The stove stood freshly blackened, with the waved white sand on its polished pipe.[10] Over the door of the bedroom steps hung the glass case with the waxen image of Our Lady, a girlish figure clad in broad white folds, with bright-red, cherry cheeks, smiling sweetly upon a doll which she carried in her arms. On the other wall was a glaring framed print, in which a Child Jesus romped with curly-headed angels in a motley green wood, with behind it a sunny perspective gleaming with paradisian delights.

[10] The Flemish stove is connected with the chimney by a flat pipe, on which the plates and other utensils are heated. On Sundays, the stove, the pipe and all are blacked and polished with black-lead and turpentine; and it is an old custom of neat house-wives to powder the stove-pipe with white sand from the dunes. The sand is allowed to run through a little opening in the hand in a series of fine wavy lines, forming a delicate pattern on the black pipe.

From the ceiling, in a white cage, hung the canary, which hopped from one perch to the other, all day long, without ever singing. On the window-seat, behind the little curtains, blossomed tall geraniums and phlox, which, through the mesh of the muslin curtains, sent a blissful fragrance through the room.

Life went its monotonous gait, measured by the slow tick of the hanging clock, that big, stupid, laughing face which so pitilessly turned its two unequal fingers round and round. Outside, close by, went the steel blows of the smith's hammer or the biting file that grated against her wall.

The sun that laughed so pleasantly through the windows and came and put all those things in a white gleaming light beamed right through into her little white soul: it was yet like that of a child, had remained innocent, never been soiled or troubled; and, now that the bad storm-time was over, it lay still in the passionless restfulness of waning life, quite taken up with all manner of harmless occupations, devotions and acquired ways of an old, god-fearing woman-person. Her face, which was wreathed in a round white goffered cap, had the smooth, yellow, waxen pallor of the statue of Our Lady, in church, and her features the severe, sober kindliness of nuns'. She was dressed in modest, stiffly-falling folds of unrumpled lilac silk, like the queens in old prints.

She spent those long, quiet days at her lace-pillow. That was her only amusement, her treasure: this half-rounded arch of smooth, blue paper on the wooden pillow-stool, occupied by a swarm of copper pins, with coloured-glass heads, and of finely-turned wooden bobbins, with slender necks and notched bodies, hanging side by side from fine white threads or heaped up behind a steel bodkin. All this array of pins, holes, drawers and trays had for her its own form and meaning, a small world in which she knew her way so well. Her deft white fingers knew how to throw, change, catch and pick up those bobbins so nimbly, so swiftly; she stuck her pins, which were to give the thread its lie and form, so accurately and surely; and, under her hand, the lace grew slowly and imperceptibly into a light thread network, grew with the leaves and flowers of her geraniums and phlox and the silent course of time.

'Twas quite a feast when, in the evening, she wound off the ravelled end and carefully examined the white web. She closely followed all the knots, curves and twists of those transparent little veins; and 'twas with regret that she rolled up the lace again and put it away in the drawer.

When all her peaceful thoughts had been fully pondered, when all that life of every day, all that even round of happenings, like little white flakes floating in the sunny sky, had drifted by through the thought-chambers of her soul and when the light began to fail out of doors and in, she took her rosary and prayed, for hours on end, slowly telling the smooth beads between her fingers until, when it grew quite dark, she started awake and became aware that for some time she had been telling the strokes of the smith's hammer on the other side of the wall. Then she laid herself between the white sheets and tried to sleep.

Two days ago the grid of her stove broke and today she had taken it to be mended; she had been to the smith's and now she could not get out of her mind what she had seen there: a black cave, like an oven, down three steps; a dark hole hung and filled on every side with black iron tools; and, amid all this jumble, an anvil and, in the red glow from the dancing light of the smithy fire, a small, stunted, black little fellow, hidden out of knowledge in that gloom; a bent, thin little man wound in a leathern apron and with a black face, from which a pair of good-humoured eyes peered out at her, through the shining glasses of his copper-rimmed spectacles, like two little lights in the dark. She had gone down those three steps, looking round shyly, afraid of getting dirty; had explained her business to that impish little chap; and had then hastily fled from that hell. Now it seemed to her that those two eyes had looked at her so kindly; and she wondered how any one could live in such a hole and be a Christian creature ... and yet that smith looked as if he had a good heart.

Next day, she was thinking again of the little man and his dark, haunted hole; and she sniffed the scent of her geraniums with a new pleasure and looked with more gladness at her trim little dwelling and her lace-pillow. She now enjoyed, realized, with all the sensual luxury of her soul, that peaceful life of hers, something like that of the yellow, waxen Virgin high up there on the wall, under her glass shade. And yet she was sorry for her good neighbour: it must be so dreary alone, amid all that dirt.... She worked at her lace, prayed and tried to think of nothing more.

He brought the new grid home himself. At first, she was shy with the man: she got up, went to the stove, turned back again and only now and then dared look at the smith from under her eyes. He was wrapped up in his work, stood bending over the stove, trying to fix the grid. Seen like that in the light, the little chap looked quite different to her eyes: he was no longer young, his breath came quickly; but in all that he did there was something so friendly, so kindly, something almost well-mannered, that went oddly with his dirty clothes and his black face. The little smith was known in the village as a lively person, who led a lonely life, but who was able also to divert a company: he knew his customers and knew how to manage them all. Here he took good care not to dirty the floor: he spat his tobacco-juice into the coal-box and touched nothing with his hands. When at last the grid was fixed, he stayed talking a little: he spoke of her nice little life among all those white things; paid her a compliment on her pretty flowers and shining copper; and then came close to look at her lace-pillow. Lastly, seeing that she was not at her ease, that she answered his remarks so shortly and hesitatingly, he gave a push to his cap, refused to say what she owed him and was gone with a skip and a jump.

One Sunday, after vespers, he came again, bowed politely, fetched a bit of paper out of his waistcoat-pocket and sat down on a chair by the stove. This visit annoyed her: with the quickness with which small-minded people weigh and think over a matter, her eyes went to the window to see if anybody had observed him come in and was likely to set evil tongues a-clacking. It was almost bound to be so; and, to keep her honour safe, she opened her door, mumbling something about "warm weather" and "the tobacco-smoke which made her cough."

She went to her room, fetched some money and paid the bill. The smith sat where he was, knocked out his little stone pipe and put it in his inside pocket; he did not look at his money and, in his hoarse little voice, began to talk of quite common things: of wind and weather and the current news of the village; always chatting in the same tone, a jumble of long, breathless statements. From this he went on to his dreary, lonely life, the monotonous quiet of it and the danger of thieves, sickness and sudden death. She said not a word, but, against the bright window-curtains, the sharp, heavy profile of her face, together with the flutes of her white cap, went up and down in a continual nodding assent to everything he said. At the end, she took pleasure in hearing him talk, nor now looked upon that clean-washed face of his as at all so ugly. It even did her good to see some one sitting there who came to enliven the monotony of that long Sunday evening. By her leave, he had lighted a fresh pipe; and she now sat sniffing up that unaccustomed smell, which rose in little puffs from behind the stove and floated round the room, filling it with long rows of blue curls. 'Twas as if she were overcome by that quite new smell of tobacco and she felt inclined to sleep; she stood up, to get rid of that slackness, shut the front-door and, without thinking what she was doing, asked if he would have some coffee. He nodded, gladly.

She put the kettle on and got the coffee-pot ready, fetched out her best cups and spoons and the white sugar. When the steam came rushing from the spout, she poured water on the coffee and they sat down, one on each side of the table, to sip the savoury drink in tiny draughts. 'Twas long since she had felt so comfortable and for the first time she thought with dislike of her lonely life. 'Twas late when he went home; she came with him to the door ... and saw black figures that strolled past in the street and perhaps had seen him leave. She had bad dreams all night: the people pointed their fingers at her and slanderous tongues spread ugly things about her. The whole of the next day her thoughts were in the smithy; she swept the pavement more carefully and farther than usual, went now and then and looked out of window; and her little curtains were left open with a split in the middle. Yesterday, she had forgotten to give the canary fresh water to drink. The people looked at her in the street; two or three god-fearing gossips had let her walk home alone. This gave her great pain; 'twas as though a heavy load were weighing day and night on her breast; and yet she was not sorry for what had happened. All these trifles could not make her forget her content. She said her prayers and performed her little duties with as much care as before and lived on, alone.

On Sunday, she went to church very early and prayed

long: it did her so much good, that delightful whispering with God, that sweet kind Lord Who listened to her so patiently and always sent her away with fresh courage, strengthened to walk on bravely along life's irksome way. Sometimes she was frightened at her behaviour! She was gnawed by a reproachful thought: that she had left the straight path, that she no longer lived for God alone, that she was forgetting her dear saints and busy with sinful thoughts. And yet, when she carefully considered everything, nothing had happened that seemed to her blameworthy; all that change in her life had come as of itself and in spite of herself; and really, after all, there was no harm in it. She prayed for that good man, who certainly needed her spiritual aid: he went so seldom to church and lived in such a dreary black hole. Her prayers and interest would for sure bring him to a better frame of mind. And yet she must watch, keep strong, avoid the dangers: her honour was a tender thing; and people were wicked. She stayed longer than usual in the confessional and offered special prayers to every saint in the church.

When she was back at home, she began her little Sunday duties: the lace-pillow was put away that day and she did nothing but arrange things, put things in their places, gather a fresh nosegay for the porcelain vase before Our Lady's statue and see to her cooking. She picked the withered leaves from the geraniums, bound the branches of the phlox to the trellis and gave them fresh water from a little flowered can. She was specially fond of her little pot of musk: it stood on the window-seat, opposite her chair, carefully set in a rush cage stuck into the earth and fastened at the top with a thread. Sometimes she took it on her lap, bent her face over it and sniffed the pleasant smell in long draughts, until she was almost drunk with it.

In the afternoon, she sat down at the window and read her Thomas a Kempis. Then all was quite still: no hammering behind the wall, no boys in the street, only the soft tapping of the canary in his food-trough and the tick of the pendulum; everything was quiet as though in an enchanted sleep. The sun glowed through the geranium-leaves and cast on the red-tiled floor a broad, round shadow which took the whole afternoon to creep from the legs of the stove to the front-door.

The flies buzzed round on the rafters of the ceiling or ran along the cracks of the white-scoured table. Her thoughts wandered wearily and lazily through the wise maxims of her book and she sometimes sat peering at the funny shape of a coloured initial which, after long looking, became such a silly figure, one that no longer looked in the least like a letter, but was rather something in the form of a vice.... The lines of print ran into one another, the maxims said all sorts of foolish things, her eyes closed, her head nodded and she sank, with all those peaceful things, into perfect rest.

After dinner, the smith had had a sleep; then he washed his face, put on his best clothes and went past her window to vespers. In the evening, she saw him again when he went to the customers for a pot of beer: this time he gave her a friendly nod.

For her, Sunday passed like all the other days; she prayed longer and closed her shutter earlier for fear of the drunkards. After saying a long row of graces which she knew by heart, she went to her bedroom. In the stuffy air of that closed upper chamber, she lay thinking. She was not sleepy and it was nice, in the evening stillness, covered in her white sheets, to lie with her eyes looking through the split in the white curtains at the moon which hung shining outside.

Now she gave free scope to her thoughts, until all of that had again been pondered round and pondered out. Then it became so funny to her: 'twas as if she were long dead now and floating in a pale and scented air in the company of sweet saints and angels. But it was oh, so hazy and indistinct! It always escaped her when she wanted to enjoy it more closely and to give the thing a name.

It was night when the smith came home, a little tipsy, deceived by his great thirst and the double effect of the beer in that warm weather. He was very cheery, without really knowing why; something like a soft buzzing fire ran through all his body and made him tingle with happiness. They had chaffed him that evening about the old maid next door and he now felt inclined just to tell her about it.

Wasn't it a shame for two people to lie here so quietly and drearily, parted by a bit of a wall, when they could have been amusing each other?... His white neighbour was sure to be asleep by now ... and, if he only dared ... and, quicker indeed than he intended, he gave three little taps on the wall and lay listening, all agog.... Three like little taps answered! This was so unexpected that at first he sat wondering whether he could believe his ears; then he began to swim and sprawl in his bed, bit his teeth so as not to shout out his overflowing delight and started banging on the wall, this time with his fists. It was too late to-night: to-morrow, he would go to her and ask her ... and then they would both ...

and he would no longer be alone, always alone, and would have some one to care for him, to look after him.... In all this happiness he drowsed off gently, rocked in another world, like a little wax doll in a pale-blue paper box.

She had started out of her sleep at those three taps and had answered, not knowing why; then she had got frightened at that wild man behind her wall, had jumped out of bed and struck a light and sat waiting until the noise stopped; then she commended her soul into the Lord's hands and fell softly asleep.

The first time that he went to see her, he found the door shut. Once, when he met her in the street, she kept her eyes carefully cast down and passed him without a sign of greeting. Her curtains remained drawn and she never came to the door now. He went home and sat musing on his anvil. All his plan was blown to bits; he found himself sadly duped and turned red with anger when folk spoke of his dear neighbour. He hammered and filed from morning till night; and she must now be making her lace.

Time pushed past, divided into even days, along a smooth road that led down the mountain-slope of summer. The leaves fell from the geraniums and the phlox. The neatly-cut-out paper fly-catcher was put away and the lamp hung up in its place. With the sad, short days came the grey, misty sky, the dismal, dripping rain and the white snow. The village lay dead for half the day, dark, with here and there a little ray of light gleaming through the shutters.

And it became gradually drearier for her: that calm rest, in which she had once found such a pure delight, was now a heavy weariness. She longed for change, for something different which she could not justly define, or else to live again as before, alone and with nothing but herself. She had struggled and fought to rid herself of that obsession, but it followed her everywhere: she saw him go by, even when her eyes were fixed on the lace-pillow, the stove, or the chair on which he had sat; and there was that constant hammering and scratching behind her wall: everywhere she saw those two kind eyes behind the copper rims of his spectacles; and she sometimes caught herself contentedly tracing the good-natured features of his little black face. She had prayed more than ever and evoked quite new saints; and now she let herself drift along at God's pleasure, no longer even thinking of her weakness. Perhaps she was the instrument of a Blessed Providence, destined blindly to do good.

The little curtains had long been pushed apart again; and, each time that she heard approaching footsteps, her heart went beating and her eyes looked eagerly to see if by chance ... it was not he.

Sometimes, an anxious fluttering drove her to the front-door, where she stood looking round for a while and then, ashamed of herself, went indoors again. Quite against her habit, she now made use of her glass: in the middle of her work, she went to see if the two glossy black tresses lay neatly on her forehead and if the ribbons of her cap were properly tied and fastened. She put on her clothes more carefully and folded and refolded her kerchief till it enclosed her body in a pretty shape. From before the moment of starting for church, her heart began to beat; she shut her garden-gate more noisily and stepped loudly along the pavement until she came to the smith's first window, firmly resolved this time at least to look up and say good-morning; but she always met some one who noticed her; and she was in church by the time that, with a sigh, she had put off her intention until next day.

At night, in bed, she lay thinking over all these little events; and it was a glad day or a sad day for her according as she had more or less often caught sight of the little smith.

One evening, after benediction, she saw him come walking under the trees of the churchyard. Not a soul saw them. Now she really must have courage; but again the blood came to her throat and she felt that once again it would lead to nothing. He had just looked round before she came up to him and then he sat down on the stone step before the Calvary, as though he wanted to chat with her there at his ease:

"Good-evening, Sofie," he said, with a smile. "Have you been to say your prayers. Don't you ever say a little one for me? I want it so badly: my soul's as black as my apron and I can't even read a prayer-book...."

He made all this speech in a soft, fondling little tone and then sat smirking to see what she would say. There was nothing that she longed for more than to save his soul:

"Can you say the Rosary?" she asked.

"Yes, but I haven't one."

"Would you like me to give you one?"

"Oh, rather ... if you'll be so good!"

She bent close to him and whispered in his ear:

"Come and fetch it, to-morrow evening, when it's dark."

They walked together through the peaceful twilit churchyard and, with a cordial "Good-evening," went home well pleased with themselves.

For her it was an endless day; all the time she stood considering what she should say to him. He was coming and would sit smoking there again behind the stove. Already she heard his pleasant, whispering talk and saw his kind, upturned glance. She moved about restlessly to set everything in order. The shutters were closed quite early and the lamp burning. Now she went and had one more look outside and it was pitch-dark, with never a moon. On the stroke of eight, the door opened: he was there, with his Sunday jacket on, his red scarf and his leather shoes. She was most friendly, but did not at first know how to begin the conversation.

He lit his pipe and snuffled some news of the village and of people who were married, sick or dead. She made coffee, turned up the lamp and opened her bedroom door to give an outlet to the tobacco-smoke. Straight opposite him, deep in the half-darkness, he saw all that show of white: against the wall stood the bed, under a white canopy of curtains hanging in folds, set off with a white ball-fringe; also a praying-desk with velvet cushions, above which was an image of the Sacred Heart, with gold flowers, and, hanging from a brass chain, a perpetual light glimmering in a little red glass; and, all around, on the white walls, little statues and pictures, like a devout little tabernacle ashine with cleanliness. They drank their fragrant cup of coffee and nibbled lumps of white sugar.

"And my rosary?" he asked.

She fetched it out of the drawer of her lace pillow and came and sat close to him to teach him how to say it:

"Here, at the little cross, the I Believe in God the Father; then, at each big bead, an Our Father; and, at the little ones, a Hail Mary."

He sat with his legs drawn under his chair, with one hand at his chin, listening good-humouredly and, with a smile, repeating all she taught him. Her eyes shone with happiness. Now the talk went easily on church matters and all the things of her pious little life; she showed him the pictures in her prayer-book, explained all the attributes of the saints and told long stories of their lives and martyrdoms.

He, also, told her of his youth, when he made his first communion and was the best little man in the whole village. It was striking ten when he went home; and he had promised to come and listen to her again.

Every evening, when it grew dark, he sat peeping to see if there was no one in the street and then cautiously crept in through her gate. He brought her old books from his loft; and, while he smoked his pipe, she lit the candle before the statue of Our Lady and started talking, very gently, so as not to be heard outside. She read whole chapters out of Thomas a Kempis and *The Pious Pilgrim*, *The Dove amongst the Rocks*, *The Spiritual Bridegroom*, or *The Sacred Meditations*. They sat there for hours at a time gazing at each other and smiling. When it grew late, she went and looked outside and, when the moment was favourable, she carefully let him out. She thanked Our Lord for making her so happy and often prayed that it might last and she win the smith's soul for Heaven and that their doing might all the same be kept hidden from wicked people.

St. Eloi's Day is the holiday of smiths and husbandmen. In the morning, the farmers all went together to mass and thence, after a glass, to settle their yearly reckoning at the smith's. At noon there was a big dinner at the inn. They ate much and drank more; and, from afternoon till late in the evening, the smiths' men and the peasants loafed along the streets and sang ribald songs. The steadiest of them walked about talking, from one tavern to the other. They were nearly all drunk. She sat peeping at it from behind her curtain and was vexed at all this wantonness and rather glad that she had not yet seen "him" anywhere. She said her evening prayers and was just going to bed when she heard the door open and the smith stepped in.

He carried his pipe upside down in his mouth, his eyes looked wild and his speech was incoherent. She had never seen him like that; and she was frightened at his strange gestures. She wanted him to sit down, but he came up to her with his arms open, as if to catch hold of her. She stepped back in affright, pushed him away from her. His breath stank of drink and his thin legs tottered under him. She began to beseech him, that it was late and that he should go home and that people would know.... But his eyes looked at her roguishly and, with bent head and outstretched arms, he kept on trying to come closer. Filled with dread, she wavered away behind the tables and chairs, whimpering:

"If you please, if you please, Sander, go home; you frighten me!"

Suddenly, he nipped out the flame of the lamp with his fingers. It was quite dark.

"Sander! Sander! What do you want? Heavens! He's drunk! And I'm here all alone! Lord God, St. Catherine, help!"

He still spoke not a word, but uttered ugly growls; and she heard his hands rub and grope along the wall, against herself. She pulled open the door of her bedroom and fled up the stairs and fell in a heap in the corner beside her bed. There she sat waiting, out of breath.... Yes, his heavy shoes had found the steps; and, still growling, he entered the room. He felt the bed, lay down flat on his stomach and reached out with his arms; then he found her sitting sighing. She felt those two weedy arms grasp her and was caught in them as in an iron band. She moaned and screamed for help. His dirty, slimy mouth pressed her lips ... and then she felt herself sink away, out of the world. The people who heard the cries came to see what was the matter. They hauled the drunkard outside and laid her on the bed. When they saw that she was better, they went away again.

She lay stretched out slackly in the dark. First, still quite overcome, as though drunk with sleep, she slowly, through that dim whirl of stormy thoughts, came to understand what had happened: all her misfortune, which yawned before her like a deep, black well. She was ashamed, disgusted with herself and felt a great aversion, a loathing for all the world: people were a pack of lustful pigs.... And he too: that was over now, suddenly over, for good and all.... And he ... no, he had deceived her, grievously defiled her. And now to have to go on living like that! It was done past recall: she was punished for her trustfulness ... and those same kind eyes and that friendly face; only yesterday, they had said their evening prayers together and so devoutly! Oh, 'twas such a pity! And what would people say?... And the priest?... And Our Lord and all His dear saints?... She fell into ever-deepening despair and saw never a way out. Very far away shone her pure little life of former days, her white and peaceful little soul floating in that unruffled blue sanctity, in that fragrant twilight of evening after evening ... and all this he had now crushed in one second and stamped to pieces. And he was dead to her, he with whom she had dreamed so sweetly and lived in glad expectation. In her wretchedness, she was left stark alone, abandoned like a poor babe in the snow. She plunged her face into the white sheets and cried. She would have liked to pine away there, in that kindly darkness, and never, never to see daylight again.

XI

THE END

Zeen pulled up his bent back, wiped the sweat from his forehead with his bare arm and drew a short breath.

Zalia, with her head close to the ground, went on binding her sheaves.

The sun was blazing.

After a while, Zeen took up his sickle again and went on cutting down the corn. With short, even strokes, with a swing of his arm, the sickle rose and, with a "d-zin-n-n" fell at the foot of the cornstalks and brought them down in great armfuls. Then they were hooked away and dragged back in little even heaps, ready to be bound up.

It did not last long: he stopped again, looked round over all that power of corn which still had to be cut and beyond, over that swarming plain, which lay scorching, so hugely far, under that merciless sun. He saw Zalia look askant because he did not go on working and, to account for his resting, drew his whetstone from his trouser-pocket and began slowly to sharpen the sickle.

"Zalia, it's so hot."

"Yes, it's that," said Zalia.

He worked on again, but slowly, very slackly.

The sweat ran in great drops down his body; and sometimes he felt as if he would tumble head foremost into the corn. Zalia heard his breath come short and fast; she looked at him and asked what was the matter. His arms dropped feebly to his sides; and the hook and sickle fell from his hands.

"Zalia, I don't know ... but something's catching my breath like; and my eyes are dim...."

"It's the heat, Zeen, it'll wear off. Take a pull."

She fetched the bottle of gin from the grass edge of the field, poured a sip down his throat and stood looking to see how it worked:

"Well?"

Zeen did not answer, but stood there shivering and staring, with his eyes fixed on a bluebonnet in the cut corn.

"Come, come, Zeen, get it done! Have just another try: it'll get cooler directly and we'll be finished before dark."

"Oh, Zalia, it's so awfully hot here and it'll be long before it's evening!"

"But, Zeen, what do you feel?"

Zeen made no movement.

"Are you ill?"

"Yes, I am, Zalia. No, not ill, but I feel so queer and I think I ought to go home."

Zalia did not know what to do: she was frightened and did not understand his funny talk.

"If you're ill ... if you can't go on, you'd better get home quick: you're standing there like a booby."

Zeen left his sickle on the ground and went straight off the field. She saw him go slowly, the poor old soul, lurching like a drunken man, and disappear behind the trees. Then she took her straw-band and bundled up all the little heaps of corn, one after the other, and bound them into sheaves. She next took the sickle and the hook and just went cutting away like a man: stubbornly, steadily, with a frenzied determination to get it done. The more the corn fell, the quicker she made the sickle whizz.

The sweat ran down her face; now and then, she jogged back the straw hat from over her eyes to see how much was left standing and then went on cutting, on and on. She panted in the doing of it.... She was there alone, on that outstretched field, in that heat which weighed upon her like a heavy load; it was stifling. She heard no sound besides the swish of her steel and the rustling of the falling corn.

When at last she could go on no longer, she took a sip at the bottle and got new strength.

The sun was low in the sky when she stood there alone on the smooth field, with all the corn lying flat at her feet. Then she started binding.

The air grew cooler. When the last sheaf was fastened in its straw-band and they now stood set up in heavy stooks, like black giants in straight rows, it began to grow dark. She wiped the sweat from her face, slipped on her blue striped jacket, put the bottle in her hat, took the sickle and hook on her shoulder and, before going, stood for a while looking at her work. She could now see so very far across that close-shorn plain; she stood there so alone, so tall in that stubble-field, everything lay so flat and, far away over there, the trees stood black and that mill and the fellow walking there: all as though drawn with ink on the sky. It seemed to her as if the summer was now past and that heavy sultriness was a last cramped sigh before the coming of the short days and the cold.

She went home. Zeen was ill and it was so strange to be going back without him. It was all so dreary, so dim and deadly, so awful. Along the edge of the deep sunken path the grasshoppers chirped here and there, all around her: an endless chirping on every side, all over the grass and the field; and it went like a gentle woof of voices softly singing. This singing at last began to chatter in her ears and it became a whining rustle, a deafening tumult and a painful laughter. From behind the pollard her cat jumped on to the path: it had come to the field to meet her and, purring cosily, was now arching its back and loitering between Zalia's legs until she stroked it; then it ran home before her with great bounds. The goat, hearing steps approach, put its head over the stable-door and began to bleat.

The house-door was open; as she went in, Zalia saw not a thing before her eyes, but she heard something creaking on the floor. It was Zeen, trying to scramble to his feet when he heard her come in.

"Zeen!" she cried.

"Yes," moaned Zeen.

"How are you? No better yet? Where are you?... Why are you lying flat on the floor like this?"

"Zalia, I'm so ill ... my stomach and...."

"You've never been ill yet, Zeen! It won't be anything this time."

"I'm ill now, Zalia."

"Wait, I'll get a light. Why aren't you in bed?"

"In bed, in bed ... then it'll be for good, Zalia; I'm afraid of my bed."

Shc felt along the ceiling for the lamp, then in the corner of the hearth for the tinder-box; she struck fire and lit up.

Zeen looked pale, yellow, deathlike. Zalia was startled by it, but, to comfort him:

"It'll be nothing, Zeen," she said. "I'll give you a little Haarlem oil."

She pulled him on to a chair, fetched the little bottle, put a few drops into a bowl of milk and poured it down his throat.

"Is it doing you good?"

And Zeen, to say something, said:

"Yes, it is, Zalia, but I'd like to go to sleep, I'm feeling cold now and I've got needles sticking into my side ... here, see?"

And he pressed both his hands on the place.

"Yes, you're better in bed; it'll be gone in the morning and we'll fetch in the corn."

"Is it cut?"

"All done and stooked; if it keeps fine to-morrow, we'll get it all into the barn."

Zalia lifted him under his armpits and they crawled on like that into the other room, where the loom stood with the bed behind it. She helped him take off his jacket and trousers and put him to bed, tucked him nicely under the blanket and put his night-cap on his head.

Then she went and lit the fire in the hearth, hung up the pot with the goat's food, washed the potatoes and sat down to peel them for supper.

She had not peeled three, when she heard Zeen bringing up.

"That's the oil, it'll do him good," she thought and, fetching a can of water from outside, gave him a bowl to drink.

Then she went back to her peeling. A bit later, she sat thinking of other remedies - limeflowers, sunflower-seeds, pearl barley, flowers of sulphur - when suddenly she saw Mite Kornelje go by. She ran out and called:

"Mite!"

"What is it, Zalia?"

"Mite, Zeen is ill."

"What, ill? All at once?"

"Yes, all of a sudden, cutting the corn in the field."

"Is he bad?"

"I don't know, I've given him some Haarlem oil, he's been sick; he's complaining of pains in his side and in his stomach; he's very pale: you wouldn't know him."

They went indoors. Zalia took the lamp and both passed in, between the loom and the wall by Zeen's bed.

He lay staring at the ceiling and catching his breath. Mite stood looking at him.

"You must give him some English salt,[11] Zalia."

[11] Epsom salts.

"Why, Mite, I never thought of that; yes, he must have some English salt."

And she climbed on to a chair and took from the plank above the bed a dusty calabash full of little paper bags and packets.

She opened them one by one and found canary-seed, blacklead, washing-blue, powdered cloves, cinnamon, sugar-candy, burnt-ash ... but no English salt.

"I'll run home and fetch some, Zalia."

"Yes, Mite, do."

And Mite went off.

"Well, Zeen, no better yet?"

Zeen did not answer. She took a pail of water and a cloth, cleaned away the mess from beside the bed and then went back to peel her potatoes.

Mite came back with the English salt. Treze Wizeur and Stanse Zegers, who had heard the news, also came to see how Zeen was getting on. Mite stirred a handful of the salt in a bowl of water and they all four went to the sick man's bed. Zeen swallowed the draught without blinking. Mite knew of other remedies, Stanse knew of some too and Treze of many more: they asked Zeen questions and babbled to him, made him put out his tongue and felt his pulse, cried out at his gasping for breath and his pale colour and his dilated pupils and his burning fever. Zeen did not stir and lay looking at the ceiling. When he was tired of the noise, he said:

"Leave me alone."

And he turned his face to the wall.

Then they all went back to the kitchen. The goat's food was done. Zalia hung the kettle with water on the hook and made coffee; and the four women sat round the table telling one another stories of illness. In the other room there was no sound.

A bit later, Mite's little girl came to see where mother was all this time. She was given a lump of sugar and sat down by her mother.

"Zalia, have you only one lamp?" asked Treze.

"That's all, Treze, but I have the candle."

"What candle?"

"The blessed candle."

"We've not come to that yet: it's only that Zeen has to lie in the dark like this and we have to go to and fro with the lamp to look at him."

"Zeen would rather lie in the dark."

"I'll tell you what: Fietje shall run home and fetch something, won't you, Fietje? And say that mother is going to stay here because Zeen is dying."

Fietje went off. The coffee was ready and when they had gulped down their first bowl, they went to have another look in the room where the sick man lay.

Zeen was worse.

"We must sit up with him," said Stanse.

"For sure," said Treze. "I'll go and tell my man: I'll be back at once."

"Tell Free as you're passing that I'm staying here too," said Stanse.

"We must eat, for all that," said Zalia; and she hung the potatoes over the fire.

Then she went to milk the goat and take it its food. It was bright as day outside and quiet, so very quiet, with still some of the heat of the sun lingering in the air, which weighed sultrily. She crept into the dark goat-house, put down the pot with the food and started milking.

"Betje, Betje, Zeen is so ill; Zeen may be dying, Betje!"

She always clacked to her goat like that. Two streams of milk came clattering in turns into the little pail.

People came: Treze and Mite's little girl, with a lantern, and Barbara Dekkers, who had also come to have a look.

"I'm here," said Zalia, "I've done, I'm coming at once."

They stood talking a bit outside in the moonlight and then went in.

"Perhaps my man'll come on," said Treze. "A man is better than three women in illness; and Virginie's coming too: I've been to tell her."

"Well, well," said Barbara, "who'd ever have thought it

of Zeen!"

"Yes, friends, and never been ill in his life; and he turned seventy."

Stanse mashed the potatoes; Zalia poured a drain of milk over them and hung them over the fire again.

"Have you all had your suppers?" she asked.

"Yes," said Treze and Barbara and Mite.

"I haven't," said Stanse.

Zalia turned the steaming potato-mash into an earthen porringer and she and Stanse sat down to it. The others drank a fresh bowl of coffee.

They were silent.

The door opened and from behind the screen came a great big fellow with a black beard:

"What's up here? A whole gathering of people: is it harvest-treat to-day, Zalia? Why, here's Barbara and Mite and...."

"Warten, Zeen is ill."

"Zeen?... Ill?"

"Yes, ill, man, and we're sitting up."

Warten opened wide eyes, flung the box which he carried over his shoulder by a leather strap to the ground and sat down on it:

"Ha! So Zeen's ill... he's not one of the youngest either."

"Seventy-five."

They were silent. The womenfolk drank their coffee. Warten fished out a pipe and tobacco from under his blue smock and sat looking at the rings of smoke that wound up to the ceiling.

"Well, perhaps I've come at the right time, if that's so."

"You can help sit up."

"Have you had your supper, Warten?"

"Yes, Zalia, at the farm."

"And how's trade?" asked Stanse.

"Quietly, old girl."

They heard a moaning in the other room. Barbara lit the lantern and all went to look. Warten stayed behind, smoking.

Zeen lay there, on a poverty-stricken little bed, low down near the ground, behind the loom, huddled deep on his bolster under a dirty blanket: a thin little black chap, leaning against a pillow in the dancing twilight of the lantern. His eyes were closed and his bony face half-hidden in the blue night-cap. His breath rustled; and each puff from his hoarse throat, blowing out the thin flesh of his cheeks, escaped through a little opening on one side of his sunken lips, which each time opened and shut.

"Ooh! Ooh! Ooh!" cried Barbara.

"That's bad, that's bad," said Stanse and shook her head.

"His eyes are shut and yet he's not asleep!"

"Zeen! Zeen!" cried Mite and she pushed him back by his forehead to make him look up. "Zeen! Zeen! It's I: don't you know Mite?"

"Oof!" sighed Zeen; and his head dropped down again without his eyes opening.

"He's got the fever," said Barbara. "Just feel how his forehead's burning and he's as hot as fire."

"Haven't you poulticed him?" asked Stanse. "He wants poultices on his feet: mustard."

"We haven't any mustard and it's far to the village."

"Then he must have a bran bath, Zalia. Stanse, put on the kettle."

"Have you any bran, Zalia?"

"No, not ready; but there's maize."

"And a sieve?"

"Yes, there's a sieve."

"Hi, Warten, come and sift!"

Warten came in:

"Zeen, how are you, my boy? Oh, how thin he is! And his breath ... it's spluttering, that's bad. He'll go off quickly, Barbara, it seems to me."

"Not to-night," said Treze.

"Warten, go to the loft, take the lamp and sift out a handful of maize; Zeen must have a bran bath at once."

Warten went up the stair. After a while, they heard above their heads the regular, jogging drag of the sieve over the boarded ceiling and the fine meal-dust snowed down through the cracks, whirling round the lamp, and fell on Zeen's bed and on the women standing round.

Zeen nodded his head. They held a bowl of milk to his mouth; two little white streaks ran down from the corners of his mouth into his shirt-collar.

The sieve went on dragging. The women looked at Zeen, then at one another and then at the lantern. In the kitchen, the kettle sang drearily....

Warten came down from the loft with half a pailful of bran. Barbara poured the steaming water on it and flung in a handful of salt.

They took the clothes off the bed and pulled his feet into the bran-water. Zeen groaned; he opened his eyes wide and looked round wildly at all those people.

He hung there for a very long time, with his lean black legs out of the bed and the bony knees and shrunk thighs in the insipid, sickly-smelling steam of the bran-water. Then they lifted him out and stuck his wet feet under the bedclothes again. Zeen did not stir, but just lay with the rattle in his throat.

"What a sad sick man," said Stanse, softly.

Mite wanted to give him some food, eggs: it might be faintness.

Treze wanted to bring him round with gin: her husband had once....

"Is there any, for the night?..." asked Stanse.

"There's a whole bottle over there, in the cupboard."

Zeen opened his eyes - two green, glazed eyes, which no longer saw things - and wriggled his arms from under the clothes:

"Why don't you make the goat stop bleating?" he stammered.

They looked at one another.

"Zalia, why won't you speak to me?... And what are all these people doing here?... I don't want any one to help me die!... I and Zalia.... I and Zalia.... Look, how beautiful! Zalia, the procession's going up the wall there.... Why don't you look?... It's so beautiful!... And I, I'm the only ugly one in it...."

"He's wandering," whispered Treze.

"And what's that chap doing here, Zalia?"

"It's I, Zeen, I: Warten the spectacle-man."

His eyes fell to again and his cheeks again blew the breath through the little slit of his mouth. It rattled; and the fever rose.

"It'll be to-night," said Treze.

"Where can Virginie be? She'll come too late."

"Virginie is better than three doctors or a priest either," thought Mite.

"Zalia, I think I'd get out the candle."

Zalia went to the chest and got out the candle.

"Mother, I'm frightened," whined Fietje.

"You mustn't be frightened of dead people, child; you must get used to it."

"Have you any holy water, Zalia?"

"Oh, yes, Barbara: it's in the little pot over the bed!"

"And blessed palm?"

"Behind the crucifix."

There was a creaking in the kitchen and Virginie appeared past the loom: a little old woman huddled in her hooded cloak; in one hand she carried a little lantern and in the other a big prayer-book. She came quietly up to the bed, looked at Zeen for some time, felt his pulse and then, looking up, said, very quietly:

"Zeen's going.... Has the priest been?"

"The priest?... It's so far and so late and the poor soul's so old...."

"What have you given him?"

"Haarlem oil, English salt...."

"And we put his feet in bran water."

Virginie stood thinking.

"Have you any linseed-meal?" she asked.

"No."

"Then ... but it's too late now, any way...."

And she looked into the sick man's eyes again.

"He's very far gone," thought Mite.

"Got worse quickly," said Barbara.

Zalia said nothing; she stood at the foot of the bed, looking at her husband and then at the women who were saying what they thought of him.

"Get the blessed candle; we must pray, good people," said Virginie; and she put on her spectacles and went and stood with her book under the light.

The women knelt on low chairs or on the floor. Warten stood with his elbows leaning on the rail of the bed, at Zeen's head. Treze took the blessed candle out of its paper covering and lit it at the lamp.

Zeen's chest rose and fell and his throat rattled painfully; his eyes stood gazing dimly at the rafters of the ceiling; his thin lips were pale and his face turned blue with the pain; he no longer looked like a living thing.

Virginie read very slowly, with a dismal, drawling voice, through her nose, while Treze held Zeen's weak fingers closed round the candle. It was still as death.

"May the Light of the World, Christ Jesus, Who is symbolized by this candle, brightly light thy eyes that thou mayest not depart this life in death everlasting. Our Father...."

They softly muttered this Our Father and it remained solemnly still, with only Warten's rough grunting and Zeen's painful breathing and the goat which kept ramming its head against the wall. And then, slower by degrees:

"Depart, O Christian soul, from this sorrowful world; go to meet thy dear Bridegroom, Christ Jesus, and carry a lighted candle in thy hands. He Who...."

Then Barbara, interrupting her, whispered:

"Look, Virginie, he's getting worse; the rattle's getting fainter: turn over, you'll be too late."

Treze was tired of holding Zeen's hand round the candle: she spilt a few drops of wax on the rail of the bed and stuck the candle on it.

Zeen jerked himself up, put his hands under the clothes and fumbled with them; then he lay still.

"He's packing up," whispered Barbara.

"He's going," one of the others thought.

Virginie dipped the palm-branch into the holy water and sprinkled the bed and the bystanders; then she read on:

"Go forth, O Christian soul, out of this world, in the name of God the Father Almighty, Who created thee, in the name of Jesus Christ, the Son of the living God, Who suffered for thee; in the name of the Holy Ghost, Who sanctified thee."

"Hurry, hurry, Virginie: he's almost stopped breathing!"

The cat jumped between Zalia and Treze on to the bed and went making dough with its front paws on the clothes; it looked surprised at all those people and purred softly. Warten drove it away with his cap.

"Receive, O Lord, Thy servant Zeen into the place of salvation which he hopes to obtain through Thy mercy."

"Amen," they all answered.

"Deliver, O Lord, the soul of Thy servant from all danger of hell and from all pain and tribulation."

"Amen."

"Deliver, O Lord, the soul of Thy servant Zeen, as Thou deliveredst Enoch and Elias from the common death of the world."

"Amen."

"Deliver, O Lord, the soul of Thy servant Zeen, as Thou deliveredst...."

"I'm on fire! I'm on fire!" howled Warten. "My smock! My smock!"

And he jumped over all the chairs and rushed outside, with the others after him.

"Caught fire at the candle!" he cried, quite out of breath.

They put out the flames, pulled the smock over his head and poured water on his back, where his underclothes were smouldering.

"My smock, my smock!" he went on moaning. "Brand-new! Cost me forty-six stuivers!"

And he stood with his smock in his hands, looking at the huge holes and rents.

They made a great noise, all together, and their sharp voices rang far and wide into the still night.

Virginie alone had remained by the bedside. She picked up the candle, lit it again, put it back on the rail of the bed and then went on reading the prayers. When she saw that Zeen lay very calmly and no longer breathed, she sprinkled him with holy water for the last time and then went outside:

"People ... he's with the Lord."

It was as if their fright had made them forget what was happening indoors: they rushed in, eager to know ... and Zeen was dead.

"Stone-dead," said Barbara.

"Hopped the twig!" said Warten.

"Quick! Hurry! The tobacco-seed will be tainted!" screamed Mite; and she snatched down two or three linen bags which hung from the rafters and carried them outside.

First they moaned; then they tried to comfort one another, especially Zalia, who had dropped into a chair and turned very pale.

Then they set to work: Treze filled the little glasses; Barbara hung the water over the fire; and Warten, in his shirt-sleeves, stropped his razor to shave Zeen's beard.

"And the children! The children who are not here!" moaned Zalia. "He ought to have seen the children!"

"First say the prayers," ordered Virginie.

All knelt down and, while Warten shaved the dead man, it went:

"Come to his assistance, all ye saints of God; meet him, all ye angels of God: receiving his soul, offering it in the sight of the Most High....

"To Thee, O Lord, we commend the soul of Thy servant, that being dead to this world, he may live to

Thee; and whatever sins he has committed in this life, through human frailty, do Thou, in Thy most merciful goodness, forgive...."

"Amen," they answered.

Virginie shut her book, once more sprinkled holy water on the corpse and went home, praying as she went.

Zalia made the sign of the Cross and closed her husband's eyes; then she laid a white towel on a little table by the bed and put the candle on it and the crucifix and the holy water.

Warten and Barbara took Zeen out of the bed and put him on a chair, washed him all over with luke-warm water, put a clean shirt on him and his Sunday clothes over him; then they laid him on the bed again.

"He'll soon begin to must," said Barbara.

"The weather's warm."

"He's very bent: how'll they get him into the coffin?"

"Crack his back."

Treze looked round for a prayer-book to lay under Zeen's chin and a crucifix and rosary for his hands.

Mite took a red handkerchief and bound it round his head to keep his mouth closed. Fietje was still kneeling and saying Our Fathers.

"It's done now," said Barbara, with a deep sigh. "We'll have just one more glass and then go to bed."

"Oh, dear people, stay a little longer!" whined Zalia. "Don't leave me here alone."

"It's only," said Mite, "that it'll be light early to-morrow and we've had no sleep yet."

"Come, come," said Barbara, to comfort her, "you mustn't take on now. Zeen has lived his span and has died happily in his bed."

"Question is, shall we do as well?" said Mite.

"And Siska and Romenie and Kordula and the boys, ho are not here! They ought to have seen their father die!... The poor children, they'll cry so!"

"They'll know it in good time," said Warten.

"And where are they living now?" asked Mite.

"In France, the two oldest ... and there's Miel, the soldier ... it's in their letters, behind the glass."

"Give 'em to me," said Treze. "I'll make my boy write to-morrow, before he goes to school."

They were going off.

"And I, who, with this all, don't know where I'm to sleep," said Warten. "My old roost, over the goat-house: you'll be wanting that to-night, Zalia?"

Zalia wavered.

"Zalia could come with me," said Barbara.

"And leave the house alone? And who's to go to the priest to-morrow? And to the carpenter? And my harvest, my harvest! Yes, yes, Warten, do you get into the goat-house and help me a bit to-morrow. I shall sleep: why not?"

"*Alla*[12], come, Fietje; mother's going home."

[12] A corruption of the French *allez!*

They went; and Zalia came a bit of the way with them. Their wooden shoes clattered softly in the powdery sand of the white road; when they had gone very far, their voices still rang loud and their figures looked like wandering pollards.

In the east, a thin golden-red streak hung between two dark clouds. It was very cool.

"Fine weather to-morrow," said Warten; and he trudged off to his goat-house. "Good-night, Zalia."

"Good-night, Warten."

"Sleep well."

"Sleep well too and say another Our Father for Zeen."

"Certainly."

She went in and bolted the door. Inside it all smelt of candle and the musty odour of the corpse. She put out the fire in the hearth, dipped her fingers once more in the holy water and made a cross over Zeen. While her lips muttered the evening prayers, she took off her kerchief, her jacket and her cap and let fall her skirt.

Then she straddled across Zeen and lay right against the wall. She twisted her feet in her shift and crept carefully under the bed-clothes. She shuddered. Her thoughts turned like the wind: her daughters were in service in France and were now sleeping quietly and knew of nothing; her eldest, who was married, and her husband and the children came only once a year to see their father; and even then.... And now they would find him dead.

Her harvest ... and she was alone now, to get it in. Warten would go to the priest early in the morning and to the carpenter: the priest ought to have been here, 'twas a comfort after all; but Zeen had always been good and ... now to go dying all at once like this, without the sacraments....

Why couldn't she sleep now? She was so tired, so worn out with that reaping; and it was so warm here, so stifling and it smelt queer: what a being could come to, when he was dead!

Had she slept at all? She had been lying there so long ... and there was that smell! She wished she had sent Warten away and gone herself to lie in the goat-house; here, beside that corpse ... but, after all, it was Zeen....

The flame of the candle flickered and everything flickered with it - the loom, the black rafters and the crucifix - in dark shadow-stripes upon the wall. 'Twas that kept her awake. She sat up and blew from where she was, but the flame danced more than ever and kept on burning. Then she carefully stepped across Zeen and nipped out the candle with her fingers. It was dark now.... She strode back into bed, stepping on Zeen's leg; and the corpse shook and the stomach rumbled.

She held herself tucked against the wall, twisted and turned, pinched her eyes to, but did not sleep. The smell got into her nose and throat and it became very irksome, unbearable. And she got out of bed again, to open the window. A fresh breeze blew into the room; far away beyond, the sky began to brighten; and behind the cornfield she heard the singing beat of a sickle and the whistling of a sad, drawling street-ditty:

"They're at work already."

Now she lay listening to the whizzing beat and the rustle of the falling corn and that drawling, never-changing tune....

The funeral would be the day after to-morrow: already she saw all the troop passing along the road and then in the church and then ... all alone, home again. Zeen was dead now and she remained ... and all those children, her children, who still had so long to live, would also grow old, in their turn, and die ... ever on ... and all that misery and slaving and then to go ... and Zeen, her Zeen, the Zeen of yesterday, who was still alive then and not ill. Her Zeen; and she saw him as a young man over forty years ago: a handsome chap he was. She had lived so long with Zeen and had known him so well, better than her own self; and that he should now be lying there beside her ... cold ... and never again ... that he should now be dead.

Then she broke down and wept.

Choose from Thousands of 1stWorldLibrary Classics By

Adolphus WilliamWard
Aesop
Agatha Christie
Alexander Aaronsohn
Alexander Kielland
Alexandre Dumas
Alfred Gatty
Alfred Ollivant
Alice Duer Miller
Alice Turner Curtis
Alice Dunbar
Ambrose Bierce
Amelia E. Barr
Andrew Lang
Andrew McFarland Davis
Anna Sewell
Annie Besant
Annie Hamilton Donnell
Annie Payson Call
Anton Chekhov
Arnold Bennett
Arthur Conan Doyle
Arthur Ransome
Atticus
B. M. Bower
Basil King
Bayard Taylor
Ben Macomber
Booth Tarkington
Bram Stoker
C. Collodi
C. E. Orr
C. M. Ingleby
Carolyn Wells
Catherine Parr Traill
Charles A. Eastman
Charles Dickens
Charles Dudley Warner
Charles Farrar Browne
Charles Ives
Charles Kingsley
Charles Lathrop Pack
Charles Whibley
Charles Willing Beale
Charlotte M. Braeme
Charlotte M.Yonge
Clair W. Hayes
Clarence Day Jr.
Clarence E. Mulford
Clemence Housman
Confucius
Cornelis DeWitt Wilcox
Cyril Burleigh
D. H. Lawrence
Daniel Defoe
David Garnett
Don Carlos Janes
Donald Keyhole
Dorothy Kilner
Dougan Clark
E. Nesbit
E.P.Roe
E. Phillips Oppenheim
Edgar Allan Poe
Edgar Rice Burroughs
Edith Wharton
Edward J. O'Biren
John Cournos
Edwin L. Arnold
Eleanor Atkins
Elizabeth Cleghorn
Gaskell
Elizabeth Von Arnim
Ellem Key
Emily Dickinson
Erasmus W. Jones
Ernie Howard Pie
Ethel Turner
Ethel Watts Mumford
Eugenie Foa
Eugene Wood
Evelyn Everett-Green
Everard Cotes
F. J. Cross
Federick Austin Ogg
Ferdinand Ossendowski
Francis Bacon
Francis Darwin
Frances Hodgson Burnett
Frank Gee Patchin
Frank Harris
Frank Jewett Mather
Frank L. Packard
Frederick Trevor Hill
Frederick Winslow Taylor
Friedrich Kerst
Friedrich Nietzsche
Fyodor Dostoyevsky
Gabrielle E. Jackson
Garrett P. Serviss
Gaston Leroux
George Ade
Geroge Bernard Shaw
George Ebers
George Eliot
George MacDonald
George Orwell
George Tucker
George W. Cable
George Wharton James
Gertrude Atherton
Grace E. King
Grant Allen
Guillermo A. Sherwell
Gulielma Zollinger
Gustav Flaubert
H. A. Cody
H. B. Irving
H. G. Wells
H. H. Munro
H. Irving Hancock
H. Rider Haggard
H. W. C. Davis
Hamilton Wright Mabie
Hans Christian Andersen
Harold Avery
Harold McGrath
Harriet Beecher Stowe
Harry Houidini
Helent Hunt Jackson
Helen Nicolay
Hendy David Thoreau
Henrik Ibsen
Henry Adams
Henry Ford
Henry Frost
Henry James
Henry Jones Ford
Henry Seton Merriman
Henry Wadsworth
Longfellow
Henry W Longfellow
Herbert A. Giles
Herbert N. Casson
Herman Hesse
Homer
Honore De Balzac

Horace Walpole
Horatio Alger, Jr.
Howard Pyle
Howard R. Garis
Hugh Lofting
Hugh Walpole
Humphry Ward
Ian Maclaren
Israel Abrahams
J.G.Austin
J. Henri Fabre
J. M. Barrie
J. Macdonald Oxley
J. S. Knowles
J. Storer Clouston
Jack London
Jacob Abbott
James Allen
James Lane Allen
James Andrews
James Baldwin
James DeMille
James Joyce
James Oliver Curwood
James Oppenheim
James Otis
Jane Austen
Jens Peter Jacobsen
Jerome K. Jerome
John Burroughs
John F. Kennedy
John Gay
John Glasworthy
John Habberton
John Joy Bell
John Milton
John Philip Sousa
Jonathan Swift
Joseph Carey
Joseph Conrad
Joseph Jacobs
Julian Hawthrone
Julies Vernes
Justin Huntly McCarthy
Kakuzo Okakura
Kenneth Grahame
Kate Langley Bosher
L. A. Abbot
L. T. Meade
L. Frank Baum
Laura Lee Hope
Laurence Housman
Leo Tolstoy
Leonid Andreyev
Lewis Carroll
Lilian Bell
Lloyd Osbourne
Louis Tracy
Louisa May Alcott
Lucy Fitch Perkins
Lucy Maud Montgomery
Lydia Miller Middleton
Lyndon Orr
M. H. Adams
Margaret E. Sangster
Margaret Vandercook
Maria Edgeworth
Maria Thompson Daviess
Mariano Azuela
Marion Polk Angellotti
Mark Overton
Mark Twain
Mary Austin
Mary Cole
Mary Rowlandson
Mary Wollstonecraft Shelley
Max Beerbohm
Myra Kelly
Nathaniel Hawthrone
O. F. Walton
Oscar Wilde
Owen Johnson
P.G.Wodehouse
Paul and Mable Thorn
Paul G. Tomlinson
Paul Severing
Peter B. Kyne
Plato
R. Derby Holmes
R. L. Stevenson
Rabindranath Tagore
Rahul Alvares
Ralph Waldo Emmerson
Rene Descartes
Rex E. Beach
Richard Harding Davis
Richard Jefferies
Robert Barr
Robert Frost
Robert Gordon Anderson
Robert L. Drake
Robert Lansing
Robert Michael Ballantyne
Robert W. Chambers
Rosa Nouchette Carey
Ross Kay
Rudyard Kipling
Samuel B. Allison
Samuel Hopkins Adams
Sarah Bernhardt
Selma Lagerlof
Sherwood Anderson
Sigmund Freud
Standish O'Grady
Stanley Weyman
Stella Benson
Stephen Crane
Stewart Edward White
Stijn Streuvels
Swami Abhedananda
Swami Parmananda
T. S. Ackland
The Princess Der Ling
Thomas A. Janvier
Thomas A Kempis
Thomas Anderton
Thomas Bailey Aldrich
Thomas Bulfinch
Thomas De Quincey
Thomas H. Huxley
Thomas Hardy
Thomas More
Thornton W. Burgess
U. S. Grant
Valentine Williams
Victor Appleton
Virginia Woolf
Walter Scott
Washington Irving
Wilbur Lawton
Wilkie Collins
Willa Cather
Willard F. Baker
William Makepeace Thackeray
William W. Walter
Winston Churchill
Yei Theodora Ozaki
Young E. Allison
Zane Grey

www.ingramcontent.com/pod-product-compliance
Lightning Source LLC
LaVergne TN
LVHW091640100826
845152LV00006B/114/J

* 9 7 8 1 4 2 1 8 0 3 9 3 7 *